THE COYOTERO KID

For two years a mysterious Apache brave, the Coyotero Kid, has been terrorizing the population of Arizona. Swooping down from the mountains to murder his victims, he vanishes again without trace. In desperation, garrison commander Colonel Bill Cummings calls in his old friend Jack Stone. Gunfighter and ex-army scout Stone is tough and resourceful and sets out on the Apache's trail. But can he succeed where the US Army and the territory's law enforcers have failed?

Books by J. D. Kincaid
in the Linford Western Library:

CORRIGAN'S REVENGE
THE FOURTH OF JULY
SHOWDOWN AT MEDICINE CREEK
COYOTE WINTER
JUDGEMENT AT RED ROCK
THE MAN WHO TAMED MALLORY
GHOST TOWN
THE LEGEND OF INJUN JOE BRADY
INCIDENT AT MUSTANG PASS
SHARKEY'S RAIDERS

J. D. KINCAID

THE COYOTERO KID

Complete and Unabridged

LINFORD
Leicester

First published in Great Britain in 2005 by
Robert Hale Limited
London

First Linford Edition
published 2006
by arrangement with
Robert Hale Limited
London

British Library CIP Data

Kincaid, J. D.
   The Coyotero Kid.—Large print ed.—
Linford western library
   1. Western stories
   2. Large type books
   I. Title
823.9'14 [F]

ISBN 1–84617–242–X

Published by
F. A. Thorpe (Publishing)
Anstey, Leicestershire

Set by Words & Graphics Ltd.
Anstey, Leicestershire
Printed and bound in Great Britain by
T. J. International Ltd., Padstow, Cornwall

1

1878

The July sun beat down relentlessly. It was hot enough to fry a rattlesnake. Brad Regan removed his sweat-stained Stetson and wiped his brow. He leant against the fence enclosing the small corral and viewed the black stallion pacing about inside it. Tough and rangy, and with a wild, untamed nature, the stallion would take some breaking. But it would be well worth the effort, for he was a fine beast and, broken in, would fetch a darned good price.

The intense heat made the air shimmer above the Arizona desert. The sagebrush, yucca, mesquite and Joshua trees seemed to dance in the haze, as did the rose-red mountains beyond. Regan narrowed his eyes, but could see little with any clarity outside the bounds of his horse ranch. He shrugged his shoulders. He did not need long-range vision in order to subdue the stallion. He smiled and began to uncoil his lariat, As he did so, a voice hailed him from behind.

'Is it OK if I watch you break in that black beauty?'

Regan turned.

'Sure, Lieutenant. Why not?' he replied amiably.

Brad Regan was a short, stocky figure, clad in his working-clothes, well-worn shirt, denim pants and boots, while the other was tall and elegant in his immaculate blue uniform. Craggy-featured and with short-cut grey hair and whiskers, Regan looked older than his forty-three years. Lieutenant Jed Lorimer, on the other hand, blond-haired, apple-cheeked and boyish, appeared much younger than his twenty-one years.

The subaltern had ridden the eight miles from Fort Bowie to the horse ranch in order to visit Regan's pretty, blue-eyed daughter, Teresa. He had met the girl during the course of the Christmas festivities, at a dance in the nearby town of Bowie. They had fallen in love and, since then, Jed Lorimer had taken every opportunity to ride over to see her. Regan and his wife had immediately taken to the young officer and, consequently, he was invariably greeted as a welcome guest. Indeed, the rancher anticipated that, in the very near future, Lieutenant Lorimer would ask him for the hand of his daughter in marriage. Sadly, however, that was not to be.

As the two men stood facing each other beside the corral, the first shot rang out. It struck the rancher in the back of the skull and exploded inside his brain, killing him instantly.

Immediately, the soldier dropped into a crouch beside his fallen friend and peered through the corral, past the still-prancing stallion and out into the shimmering haze of the desert. Apart from the sagebrush seeming to dance in the heat and the odd tumbleweed rolling across the desert floor, nothing moved. The desert appeared to be entirely devoid of man, beast or fowl. Yet someone was out there. And Lieutenant Jed Lorimer reckoned he knew who that someone was. It had to be an Apache.

In fact, there were six of them.

They emerged out of the heat haze, their small black ponies kicking up spurts of dust as they galloped towards the horse ranch. Whooping and hollering, the six young braves fired from the saddle. Lorimer stood no chance. He carried an Army Colt, whereas three of the Indians were armed with Winchesters. He was still out of range when the rifle shots struck him. Two bullets buried themselves in the ground inches from where he crouched, another sent splinters flying from the corral post directly in front of him, while the fourth and fifth hit him in the chest and knocked him flat on his back.

As Lorimer bravely attempted to rise,

4

the Apaches closed in. Two of their number sent arrows thudding into him, one in the belly and one in the shoulder. The lieutenant screamed and dropped his revolver. Then, as he clutched at the arrow protruding from his belly, the sixth Indian, a thick-set young buck who was also their leader, finished the soldier off with a pistol-shot to the head.

All this commotion had brought the other inhabitants of the horse ranch to the ranch house door. Laura Regan, a slim, middle-aged woman, with greying hair and a careworn expression, was flanked by her eighteen-year-old daughter, Teresa, and her sixteen-year-old son, Brad junior. On seeing first the rancher and then Lieutenant Lorimer cut down, both women let loose howls of anguish. Brad junior, for his part, instinctively made as though to run to the aid of his stricken father. However, an arrow through his left shoulder sent him staggering backwards into the arms of his mother and his sister.

They quickly dragged the boy inside and slammed shut the ranch house door. Thereupon, leaving Brad junior in the care of his sister, Laura Regan went and grabbed hold of the loaded shot-gun that rested on a couple of pegs driven into the wall behind her. Clutching this, she hurried across to the window next to the door. She pulled it open and looked out. But of the Apaches there was no sign. They were out of her line of vision, busily releasing the horses from the rancher's second, bigger corral and herding them at full gallop out into the desert. This had been the object of their raid, to steal the horses.

As Laura watched, one of the young bucks broke away from his fellows and galloped towards the corral containing the untamed black stallion. Laura raised the scattergun, aimed and fired. But the distance was too great. The spreading diamond pattern of ten gauge shot fell well short of its target. The Apache laughed harshly and, throwing open the gate of the corral, let loose the stallion. Then, whooping and firing his pistol into the air, the Indian drove the animal out into the desert, to join the other horses being hustled along by his five companions. Soon all that could be seen of them was a cloud of dust in the far distance.

Laura leant wearily against the window-sill, her face ashen and her eyes brimming with tears. She turned to face her son and daughter.

'Let's see to that wound,' she said.

The arrow was embedded deep in Brad junior's shoulder. Laura frowned. Would it be possible to pull the arrow straight out or might she have to cut it out? Either course of action would cause her son considerable pain, but at least the first course would be quick.

'Can . . . can you tug it out, Mother?' gasped the boy anxiously.

'I don't know, Brad,' replied Laura, 'but I can try.'

'An' if you cain't?'

'Let's not worry about that. Let's jest

try.' Laura turned to her daughter. 'Teresa, you grab hold of Brad an' hold him tight.'

'OK, Mother, I've got him,' said Teresa.

She held her brother tightly while Laura wedged a thick leather strap, part of a harness his father had been repairing, between the boy's teeth.

'Bite on that,' she instructed him.

Young Brad bit on the strap, his sister held him as tightly as she could and Laura grasped hold of the shaft of the arrow. Then suddenly, swiftly, she exerted all her strength and gave the arrow a tremendous tug. The leather strap flew out of Brad's mouth, he screamed and his mother fell backwards clutching the arrow. To her immense relief, the shaft had not broken off as she feared it might, and she stood there holding the missile, complete with its arrowhead.

A pale-faced Brad junior collapsed on to a kitchen chair. Perspiration beaded his brow. He smiled weakly.

'Thanks, Mother,' he murmured.

'OK. Sit still while I cleanse and bind your wound,' said Laura.

'I . . . I'll go see to Pa an' Jed,' said Teresa.

'No. Wait till I've finished tending Brad's wound. Then we'll go together.'

By the time Laura had tended to his wound, the colour had returned to Brad junior's cheeks and he was able to accompany the two women across the yard to the corral. Tearfully, they examined the bodies of the rancher and the subaltern. Both were stone dead.

'We must carry them into the house,' declared Laura.

'Yeah, we must,' agreed Brad junior.

'No,' said his mother. 'Teresa an' I will manage. You must ride to Fort Bowie an' report what has happened. Then, ride on into town an' fetch Horace Burton an' the Reverend Phelps.'

'Shouldn't I mebbe go fetch Mr Burton an' the reverend first?' asked the boy.

'No. There ain't no urgency regardin' the fetchin' of the mortician an' the minister, but I want the soldiers to git after them murderin' Apaches without delay.'

'OK. I'll go saddle up.'

Brad junior left his mother and sister to convey the corpses of his father and the lieutenant into the ranch house and headed for the stables.

While the raiding Indians had emptied the corral, they had not troubled to take the horses from the stables. There were just the two: a couple of elderly grey mares used to pull the Regans' buckboard.

Young Brad had to saddle one of them using only his right hand, the other arm having been temporarily rendered quite useless. Eventually, he succeeded in completing this task and climbed painfully into the saddle. Then, bidding his mother and sister goodbye, he galloped off across Arizona's sagebrush desert in the direction of Fort Bowie.

It took the youngster a little over half an hour to cover the eight miles between the horse ranch and the fort. He galloped through the open gate and up to the headquarters buildings, where he was greeted by Master-Sergeant Joe Bailey, a weather-beaten, bewhiskered veteran. The master sergeant immediately recognized Brad junior, for Brad senior had, for many years, supplied horses to the fort.

'You're in one helluva hurry, youngster,' commented Bailey, as Brad leapt out of the saddle and attempted to hitch the mare to the rail in front of him.

'I gotta see the colonel!' cried the boy.

'What is it, Brad? Is your father . . . ?'

'Pa's dead, Sergeant. Apaches killed both him an' Lieutenant Lorimer.'

'Holy cow!'

Master-Sergeant Bailey turned and, as Brad joined him on the stoop, tapped briskly upon the garrison commander's door.

'Enter!' came the cry from within.

Bailey promptly threw open the door and ushered the boy inside.

Seated behind a large mahogany desk at the far side of the office was Colonel Frederick Harriman, a big, wide-shouldered, bull-headed man in his early forties. The colonel's thick brown hair was tinged with grey at the temples, his large florid face clean-shaven. His blue eyes glittered, and his square-cut features and determined jaw gave him the appearance of having a single-minded and obdurate nature.

'Young Brad Regan to see you, sir,' announced the master sergeant, adding quickly, 'On a matter of urgency.'

The colonel ran a cold, appraising eye over the sixteen-year-old.

'Well?' he snapped.

'It — it's Pa!' exclaimed Brad. 'An' Lieutenant Lorimer.'

Harriman's interest quickened at the mention of one of his officers.

'Well?' he repeated testily.

'We've been raided by Apaches. They

— they killed Pa an' the lieutenant an' drove off our hosses.'

'When was this?'

' 'Bout half an hour back. I rode over as quick as I could. Mother said to report to you an' then ride into town to fetch Mr Burton an' the Reverend Phelps.'

'I see. How many Apaches in this raiding party?'

'Six.'

'Any idea what kinda Apaches? Tonto, or Coyotero, or Chiricahua, or . . . ?'

'No, sir.'

'OK. Doesn't matter. Sergeant, you git a coupla troopers to ride into town with the boy. An' send in Major Marshall, Captain Cummings an' Mr Stone.' Harriman smiled grimly at Brad junior. 'Don't worry, son, we'll git those bloodthirsty savages who murdered your pa. You have my word on that,' he declared.

Following the departure of the youngster and the master sergeant,

Harriman sat for a few moments, brooding on what he had been told. Lieutenant Jed Lorimer had been a good young officer, alert and keen, and Harriman was determined to track down his killers. Moreover, he intended to teach the Apaches a lesson they were unlikely to forget.

His mind was still filled with thoughts of revenge when Master-Sergeant Bailey reappeared and ushered in Major Sam Marshall, Captain Bill Cummings and Army scout, Jack Stone.

The first two wore the blue uniform of the US Cavalry, while the last-named was clad in grey Stetson, knee-length buckskin jacket and denim pants. Colonel Harriman eyed the three coolly.

The major was a few years his senior, a thin, lugubrious-looking fellow with thinning grey hair and a drooping grey moustache. Sam Marshall was a disappointed man. He had hoped to reach the rank of colonel, but had been passed over several times and now, with only two years left to serve, was resigned to the fact that he would end his career as Fort Bowie's second-in-command.

The captain, on the other hand, was in his early thirties and destined to go far. A tall, slim, dark-haired young man, Bill Cummings was both brave and smart, and had about him an air of competence.

The third man, Jack Stone, was a big, rugged-looking Kentuckian who had, in his time, been many things: deputy US marshal, sheriff, wrangler, cowboy and now, at present, he was scouting for the US Army. He had survived the Civil War and the violent years succeeding it, and was not a man to cross.

'Gentlemen,' said Harriman, 'I have some bad news. Half an hour back, a band of Apaches attacked Brad Regan's horse ranch an' murdered both him an' Lieutenant Lorimer, who happened to be visitin'.' Harriman paused while the others gasped their surprise. Then he continued: 'Their aim, it seems, was to steal Regan's horses. That bein' so, they should be easy to follow. What do you say, Mr Stone?'

'Mebbe.'

'A herd of horses must leave tracks, surely?'

'It depends. Apaches can be so goddam cunnin'. They'll do their darndest to disguise their traces. But, certainly, I'll do my best to track 'em down.'

'Good man!' Harriman turned to the two officers. 'Major, I'm gonna leave you in command of the fort. I intend to lead this expedition personally. Captain, you will turn out B Company. We ride within the hour.'

'How many Injuns are we chasin', Colonel?' enquired Stone.

'Six,' said Harriman.

Stone stared incredulously at the colonel. The man had only recently been posted to Arizona to take command of Fort Bowie and Stone had had little or no chance to assess his capabilities.

'An' you're takin' out an entire company! Surely, a troop would be sufficient?' said the Kentuckian.

'I'll decide what's sufficient, Mr Stone,' snapped Harriman. 'You go git ready to ride.'

'Yessir.'

Outside on the stoop, before heading for B Company quarters, Captain Bill Cummings addressed the Kentuckian.

'You reckon the Apache can drive off a whole herd of horses without leavin' any trace?' he demanded.

'Some Apaches can,' said Stone. 'The Chiricahua certainly can. The Coyoteros, wa'al, mebbe. They ain't always that smart. 'Deed, among the Apache tribes, they're sometimes referred to as the 'brainless ones'. Not that that applies to all of 'em.'

'No.' Cummings had had a few run-ins with the Coyotero Apache and knew them to be no mean foe. 'Let's just hope the six we're after live up to that reputation,' he said.

'Amen to that.' agreed Stone.

'Assumin', of course, that the raiders were Coyoteros an' not Chiricahua.'

He knew that Brad Regan's ranch lay on the border between Coyotero and Chiricahua lands, and so the horse thieves could easily belong to either tribe.

'We'll soon find out,' said Cummings.

'Yup.'

The captain went off to obey his colonel's order and turn out B Company. Stone, meantime, hurried off to saddle up his bay gelding.

For the next twenty minutes or so all was hustle and bustle. Then B Company drew up in columns of two, Captain Bill Cummings at the head of the first troop, and Lieutenants Andy Richards and Lewis Jones at the head of the second and third troops. The subalterns were contemporaries and close friends of the murdered Lieutenant Lorimer and, consequently, extremely anxious to avenge his death. Since Lorimer had been a popular officer with the men, the troopers were equally keen.

Colonel Harriman and Jack Stone joined Captain Cummings, and all three turned to face the open gates of the fort.

'I'll ride on ahead an' see if I can pick up the Apaches' tracks,' said Stone.

'Very good, Mr Stone,' replied Harriman.

The Kentuckian promptly set off at a gallop. As he disappeared through the gates, Harriman raised his right arm. The colonel gave the signal and thereupon B Company, with himself and Captain Cummings at their head, proceeded to ride forth. From the stoop in front of the headquarters buildings, Major Sam Marshall and Master-Sergeant Joe Bailey watched them go.

2

Jack Stone knew his limitations. He was a good enough Army scout, but no match for the Chiricahua Apache. If such were the braves who had raided the horse ranch, he stood little or no chance of tracking them down, even though they were driving a herd of horses before them. As one Army officer had so pertinently observed, chasing the Chiricahua was like 'chasing deer with a brass band'.

But Stone was lucky. When he reached the outskirts of Regan's ranch, he found the Indians had done little to disguise their traces. They had evidently made off in haste, leaving a trail that led directly up into the mountains. Once up among the rocks and the crags, however, their traces were rather less easy to follow. Yet Stone was an experienced tracker. He pursued them diligently through the chapparal of scrub oak and over sand and rock.

When, eventually, the trail ended in a deep canyon at a small Apache village, it came as no surprise to Stone that the village was occupied by Coyoteros rather than Chiricahua. The six horse thieves had certainly lived up to their reputation of being 'brainless ones'.

Stone smiled grimly and retreated from his position overlooking the canyon. He wanted to be down from the mountains and back on to the plain before darkness fell.

By maintaining a steady trot, the Kentuckian achieved this end and joined up with the pursuing B Company just as dusk was beginning to fall. He rode up to Colonel Frederick Harriman and Captain Bill Cummings at the head of the column. Immediately, Harriman raised his arm and brought his troopers to a halt.

'Well, Mr Stone?' he rasped.

'I tracked 'em to a mountain village a

few miles north of Apache Pass,' replied Stone.

'Chiricahua Apache?'

'Nope. Coyotero. The chief's Janos. He's no hothead an' not usually inclined to cause us much trouble.'

'What are you sayin', Mr Stone?'

'I'm sayin', Colonel, that I don't reckon Janos had anythin' to do with the raid on Brad Regan's ranch. Those young bucks were quite likely actin' without his say-so.'

'So?'

'So, I figure he'll hand over the miscreants who are responsible without too much fuss.'

'You reckon?'

'Yessir.'

'Yes; well, first, you have to lead us to the village.'

'Sure, but not now.' Stone gestured towards the darkening sky. 'At first light,' he said.

'Hell, they could be gone by then!'

'I don't think so, Colonel.'

'You don't think so?'

'Nope. They'd have broken camp jest as soon as those young bucks turned up with the hosses if 'n' they intended to go. The fact that they didn't indicates they feel safe from pursuit.'

'I agree with Mr Stone, sir,' interjected Cummings. 'Trackin' Apache through those mountains isn't easy. They probably figured we couldn't do it.'

'Even so.'

'I cain't guarantee to find my way back to their camp in the dark,' said Stone.

'But you're an experienced scout!'

'I'm a white man, Colonel. Only an Apache could be sure to do it at night. I need daylight to see where I'm goin'.'

'Hmmph. Perhaps the Army should recruit Apache scouts,' snorted Harriman.

'Mebbe they should,' said Stone. 'But, for now, I'm all you've got.'

'Yes. So, what do you suggest, Mr Stone?'

'That we pitch camp over there in the

foothills beside that there stream. Then, we rest up an' set out at first light. I figure we should reach their camp within a coupla hours easy.'

Colonel Harriman scowled. He was an impatient man and wanted to push on straight away. Also, being new to the territory, he did not realize how incredibly difficult was the terrain. He glanced at his subordinate.

'Mr Stone's right. If we ride up into those mountains before daybreak, we'll git lost for certain,' declared Cummings.

'Oh, very well! We pitch camp.' Harriman turned to the Kentuckian. 'But tomorrow we set off at the very first possible moment,' he snapped.

'Yessir.'

And so it was settled. Tents were pitched, campfires lit and water fetched from the stream. Stone dined on beef jerky, hard tack and coffee. Then he enjoyed a companionable cheroot and chat with B Company's two young subalterns before settling down for the night. As for Colonel Harriman and the captain, they were still earnestly discussing the day's events when Stone drifted off into a dreamless sleep.

They set off at dawn and Harriman soon discovered why Stone had refused to guide them during the hours of darkness. The trail which the Kentuckian pursued proved arduous in the extreme. They skirted crags, rode up and down the flanks of steep, almost perpendicular ridges, trotted along the ridges themselves, often no more than a foot or two wide, skeetered across huge swaths of scree and splashed through fast-flowing mountain streams. Several of the horses stumbled and a number of troopers were dislodged from their saddles. No serious injuries were sustained, however, and all succeeded in remounting. In this manner, the bluecoats, more often than not reduced to single file, plodded on in the wake of the Kentuckian until, just under two hours since breaking camp, they reached the deep canyon where the

Coyoteros had their village. B Company halted while their colonel, his officers and Stone conferred.

'See that bend,' said Stone, pointing into the mouth of the canyon. 'Their village is round there, at the far end.'

'Can you ride right through?' enquired Harriman.

'Nope. It's what is known as a box canyon,' replied Stone.

'So, those goddam savages are trapped?'

'Wa'al, not entirely. Some of 'em could climb up the sides an' escape, I s'pose.'

Harriman stared at the towering cliffs that enclosed the canyon on either side. He didn't see many Indians escaping that way.

'I think we've got them,' he stated confidently.

'Yeah. So, we ride in?'

'You're darned right we ride in. With guns blazin'.'

'But Colonel, ain't you gonna ask Janos to turn over the hoss thieves? I figure he will an' then there needn't be no bloodshed.'

'But I want blood, Mr Stone.'

'Whaddya mean?'

'I mean that I intend to teach these murderous dogs a lesson.'

'They ain't all murderin' — '

'They're savages, Mr Stone, and they have murdered an officer of the US Army. For that they shall pay.'

'There'll be women and children in the village,' interjected Captain Bill Cummings.

'That's right, Captain,' said Harriman. 'An' I want them all dead. I want the entire tribe exterminated. There will be no survivors.'

Cummings stared at his commanding officer in astonishment mixed with horror.

'But, Colonel . . . ' he began.

'Those are my orders.' Harriman turned in the saddle and addressed the two subalterns and the rest of his men. 'You hear that? We ride in there an' slaughter these stinkin' redskins, every last one of 'em. That way there'll be no chance of them murderin' any other officer in this man's army. OK?'

'Yessir,' said Lieutenant Andy Richards eagerly.

'Good! Then, let's go git 'em!'

So saying, Colonel Frederick Harriman galloped into the canyon. A reluctant, white-faced Captain Cummings, an eager Lieutenant Richards, a rather less eager Lieutenant Jones and B Company's other ranks all set off in the wake of their vengeful commander. None regarded the Apaches as other than savages. Most were happy to slaughter the Indians. Only a few had reservations about killing women and children.

One man alone determined not to participate in the attack. Jack Stone scouted for the US Army, but he was not a soldier and consequently was not obliged to join in the killing.

He turned his bay gelding's head and trotted off to where a narrow mountain path led up on to the bluffs overlooking the canyon. It was a difficult and dangerous climb, but Stone took his time and presently the gelding cantered out on to a rocky plateau. It was from this position that the Kentuckian had viewed the Apache village on the previous afternoon. Now he sat astride the gelding and watched grimly as the soldiers inflicted a terrible carnage on the village below.

The village consisted of a couple of dozen wickiups, low-domed shelters of poles lashed together with yucca fibre and covered with bear-grass and brush. These were easier and quicker to dismantle than the tepees of the Plains Indians and so ideal should the Apaches wish to break camp and disappear into the mountains in a hurry. Stone noted the horses hobbled at one end of the village, some of which were undoubtedly the ones taken from Brad Regan's ranch. He reflected that, had he been Janos, he would have ordered the abandonment of the camp the moment the bucks rode in with the stolen horses. The Coyotero chief had miscalculated badly when he had assumed they were safe from pursuit and discovery. And now he and his people were paying the price of that miscalculation.

While Stone was still climbing up the mountain path, B Company had ridden into the midst of the wickiups. Colonel Harriman reined in his horse in front of the largest of them, from which emerged a tall, broad-shouldered Coyotero Apache, a man in his early forties. The Indian was black-haired and handsome, with a proud, dignified bearing and a strong, splendidly muscled body, naked to the waist. He was Janos, chief of this sub-tribe of the Coyoteros. He raised his hand in greeting.

'Your braves have stolen the white man's horses and murdered one of my officers,' Harriman informed him.

'It was not done at my command,' stated Janos.

'But you are their chief,' retorted

Harriman and, drawing his Army Model Colt from its holster, he promptly shot the Indian twice in the chest.

Thus began the slaughter.

Before the Apaches could make a move, the troopers of B Company opened fire with their carbines. The men were cut down where they stood and then the soldiers turned their attention to the women and children. They trampled down the wickiups and set about clubbing, shooting and stabbing the defenceless squaws and their offspring. Not even babes-in-arms were spared.

Colonel Harriman and Lieutenant Richards exulted in this bloody work, using both revolver and sabre to massacre their victims. Like the majority of their men, they spared nobody. Captain Cummings and Lieutenant Jones, on the other hand, took no pleasure in the slaughter and, together with a few of the troopers, deliberately avoided killing the women and children, concentrating instead solely upon the male Apaches.

The few Apaches who survived the initial fusillade attempted either to flee past the soldiers along the canyon floor or escape up its steep, rocky sides. Not a single one of them succeeded. The former were pursued and ruthlessly cut down, while the latter were shot down as they clambered up the almost perpendicular rock-face.

At last, it was all over. Not one wickiup was left standing and the canyon was littered with dead Indians. So sudden and unexpected had been the assault that not one brave had had the chance to grab his weapon. Consequently, B Company had suffered no casualties whatsoever. Harriman was triumphant.

'That's taught those goddam savages a lesson they'll never forget!' he cried, completely ignoring the fact that, since the Apaches were all dead, they were in no position either to remember or forget what had taken place. 'But let's make sure, men. Check each an' every body. Some of the red devils could be lyin' doggo,' he added.

As the soldiers began this gory task Jack Stone retreated from the edge of the plateau. He had seen enough. Indeed, he had seen too much. The sight of so much senseless slaughter had sickened him.

The Kentuckian turned the gelding's head and trotted back towards the path up which he had recently climbed. As he did so a slight movement among a tumble of rocks a few yards to his right caught his eye. Swiftly, he dismounted, drew his Frontier Model Colt and advanced in the direction of the rocks. He stepped into the midst of them to find a young Indian boy cowering there. The boy looked to be about seven or eight years old.

There was terror in the youngster's eyes as he stared up at the big Kentuckian. Stone dropped the gun back into its holster, smiled and beckoned to the boy. The Apache's eyes opened even wider and he shrank back against the nearest boulder. He carried no weapon, but defiantly held up his small fists in defensive pose.

'I ain't gonna hurt you, boy,' said Stone softly.

This brought forth no response. The young Apache remained terrified yet defiant.

'Do you understand what I'm sayin'?'

Again there was no response, nor any sign of comprehension in the boy's huge black eyes. He continued to stare at Stone much as a jack rabbit might stare at a coyote.

'Skinya,' said Stone.

This time there was a reaction. There was a flicker in the boy's eyes indicating that he recognized the name. He should have, since Skinya was his uncle and was the chief of a neighbouring Coyotero village.

Stone pointed at the boy, then at himself and then in the direction of Skinya's village.

'I take you to Skinya,' he said.

The boy considered this proposal,

which he evidently understood. But he remained doubtful, suspicious. He shook his head.

Stone stepped across to the edge of the plateau and pointed down towards the boy's village.

'The soldiers come,' he said.

Thereupon, he turned and retreated to where his bay gelding stood idly munching a few stalks of dry grass. He remounted and held out his hand.

'Come,' he said. 'We go to Skinya.'

The boy hesitated, then, as the echoes of the troopers' final shots died away, he slowly, nervously, came forth from the tumble of boulders. He approached the Kentuckian and stood looking up at him. Stone bent low in the saddle and extended his hand towards the boy. The young Apache, with some degree of apprehension, grasped hold of it and, moments later, found himself hoisted up behind his rescuer.

Stone released the boy's hand and, digging his heels into the gelding's flanks, set off back down the narrow mountain path up which he had ridden earlier. As they embarked upon the descent, the young Apache instinctively threw his arms round Stone's waist and clung on. The climb down was no less hazardous than the climb up had been, yet they reached the plain below without mishap.

Colonel Harriman and his men remained hidden in the canyon. However, Stone realized that they would shortly reappear and he wanted to be away and out of sight before they did so. Consequently, he turned his horse's head and veered off southwards into the mountains. He did not know the actual location of Skinya's village, but he knew roughly the vicinity in which to look for it.

As luck would have it, Stone stumbled upon the village within an hour of leaving the scene of the massacre of Janos and his tribe. His arrival caused some considerable excitement, much more than he had expected. The reason for this was soon explained.

'You know that the boy you have brought here is Chie, son of Janos, and my nephew?' Skinya told him.

'No, I didn't know that,' confessed Stone.

The Coyotero chief, a tough, stocky Indian of about the same age as the deceased Janos, lifted Chie from the saddle and listened carefully while the boy told him his tearful tale. Then, handing the boy into the care of his wife, he addressed the Kentuckian. He spoke in English, which he had learned so that he might deal more easily with the white man.

'What Chie tells me is bad,' he said. 'Why do the bluecoats do this terrible thing?'

'Some of Janos's young bucks stole some hosses an', worse than that, they shot an' killed a coupla white men.'

'But did that justify massacring an entire village; men, women and children?'

'One of those killed was an officer in the US Army.' Stone sighed. 'The colonel at Fort Bowie reckoned it was justified. I don't.'

'No.' Skinya shook his head. 'It was fortunate for Chie that he was playing on the plateau up above the village when the bluecoats attacked,' he commented.

'Yup. It sure was.'

'The braves who took the horses, they were tracked to Janos's village?'

'That's right.'

'Janos was foolish. When the braves returned to the village, he should have immediately dispersed his people into the mountains.'

'My thoughts exactly.' Stone shrugged his shoulders and added: 'I s'pose I can leave the boy in your care?'

'Yes. Chie will be treated as one of my sons.'

'OK, I'll be goin', then.'

'I thank you for bringing the boy here.'

'It was the least I could do, for I ain't

too proud of the part I played in that there massacre.'

'You participated in it?'

'Nope, but I was the feller who tracked down them bucks. If 'n' I'd known what the colonel had in mind, I'd never have led him an' his men to Janos's village.'

So saying, the Kentuckian wheeled the gelding round and set off back the way he had come. Skinya watched him go, his face impassive, but his eyes blazing with suppressed fury. He wanted revenge. However, he knew that any assault upon Fort Bowie would be utter folly.

It was late afternoon when Jack Stone eventually rode through the gates of the fort. He dismounted in front of the headquarters buildings and hitched his horse to the rail outside. He was promptly confronted by Master-Sergeant Joe Bailey.

'Hell, Jack, the colonel's out for your blood!' exclaimed the sergeant. 'Reckons you deserted, leavin' him an' B

Company to find their own way back outa the mountains.'

'They made it?'

'Yeah, 'bout an hour ago.'

'OK, Joe, I'll go report to him.'

'Let me announce you.'

Bailey smiled thinly and tapped on his commanding officer's door. From inside, Colonel Harriman's voice barked the order to enter. Bailey threw open the door and stepped into the office. Harriman looked up from behind the large mahogany desk.

'Well, what is it, Sergeant?' he demanded.

'Mr Stone reportin' for duty, sir,' replied the sergeant.

'Is he, goddammit?'

'Yessir,' said Stone, stepping briskly past Bailey to confront the colonel.

'That'll be all, Sergeant,' snapped Harriman.

'Sir!'

Bailey promptly, and thankfully, saluted and withdrew.

Colonel Frederick Harriman regarded

the Kentuckian with a cold, malevolent eye, his large, florid features contorted into an angry scowl.

'Where the hell have you been?' he asked.

'Here an' there,' replied Stone coolly.

'Whaddya mean, here an' there?'

'I took a ride into the mountains.'

'You deserted your post. I needed you to guide B Company back to Fort Bowie.'

'You managed.'

'Yes, but it wasn't easy. A man could lose himself in that territory for days on end.'

'I guess so.'

'You didn't care that that could have happened to B Company?'

'Nope.'

'Goddammit! You're a darned disgrace, Stone!' Harriman bawled, adding furiously, 'I oughta have you court-martialled.'

'But I ain't one of your soldiers. I'm a civilian.'

'I'm aware of that. I cain't court-martial you, but I can sack you. I expect complete loyalty from my scouts.'

'An' I expect the Army I serve to behave like soldiers, not savages. You called me a disgrace, Colonel; wa'al, in my book it's you who's the disgrace. You're nuthin' but a stinkin', low-down murderer of defenceless women an' children.'

'Stone, how dare you? I — I — '

'Aw, shuddup! You ain't sackin me; I'm quittin'.'

With these words, the Kentuckian turned on his heel and headed towards the door.

'Stop! I haven't finished with you yet!' cried Harriman, rising from behind his desk and hastily drawing his Army Colt.

Stone stopped, his hand upon the door-handle, and glanced over his shoulder.

'You gonna shoot me in the back?' he drawled. 'I guess that's 'bout your style. I certainly don't see you facin' me man to man. That'd take guts.'

Harriman slowly lowered the revolver. He was trembling with rage.

'Git out!' he shouted.

Stone turned the door-handle and was gone.

Moments later, he rode out through the gates of Fort Bowie.

3

1888

It had been a long, hot, dusty ride across the Arizona desert and the four horsemen were mightily relieved when, eventually, they rode into the small township of Sulphur Springs on that sunny April afternoon.

Despite the heat, all four wore brown derby hats and ankle-length brown leather coats. They had ridden all the way south from Montana, but they figured that the prospect of earning $2,000 was worth the time and the trouble. They were bounty hunters who preferred to work as a team rather than alone.

Jerry Payne was their leader, a tall beanpole of a man. Raven-haired and thin-faced, with cold, expressionless grey eyes, a narrow rat-trap of a mouth and a pencil-slim black moustache, he was what he looked, namely an ice-cool, remorseless professional killer.

Payne's companions were no less deadly. Butch Mason was a huge bear of a man, heavily bearded and bewhiskered, while the cousins Norrie and Henry James looked more like brothers, both short and stocky, with ugly, pock-marked faces and piggy black eyes. Only a livid scar, running the length of his left cheek, distinguished Norrie James from his cousin.

All four men carried Remington revolvers in their holsters and Winchester rifles in their saddle boots. In addition, Jerry Payne had a large, vicious-looking Bowie knife in a sheath at his waist. The bounty hunters were not slow to draw these weapons. Their remit was to bring in desperadoes dead or alive. Invariably, they brought in their quarry dead.

They rode down Main Street until they reached the Silver Spurs saloon, where they dismounted and hitched their horses to the rail outside.

A few moments later, Jerry Payne was inside at the long, copper-topped bar ordering four beers for himself and his companions. The Silver Spurs was like one hundred other saloons across the length and breadth of the West and, since it was only mid-afternoon, there were few drinkers in the bar-room. None of its sporting women was present; they would put in an appearance later. The proprietor, who was also Sulphur Springs' mayor, was present, however, and he eyed the four strangers with some concern. Jim Byers was a pretty shrewd judge of character and he smelt trouble. He was grateful, therefore, when the town marshal, Frank Hall, strolled in. Hall had espied the bounty hunters ride into town as he sat smoking a cheroot in his rocking-chair on the stoop outside the law office, and he had decided to follow them and enquire what their business in town might be.

The two men approached the four

drinkers at the bar. Jerry Payne observed them coming. He noted that the lawman, slim and dapper in a dark grey three-piece city-style suit and derby hat, none the less looked a pretty tough *hombre*, while the mayor, fat and florid-faced in a black Prince Albert coat, scarlet vest and tall stovepipe hat, did not. Payne also noted that the former had a Colt Peacemaker strapped down on his left thigh.

'Howdy, gents,' said the marshal. 'I'm the law around here. Frank Hall's the name. An' this here's our town mayor an' the proprietor of this establishment, Mr James Byers.'

'Jim to my friends,' added the mayor, with a nervous smile.

'You boys got business here in Sulphur Springs, or are you jest passin' through?' enquired Hall.

'We got business around here, Marshal, but not actually in town,' replied Jerry Payne.

'Oh, yeah?'

'Yeah. We're bounty hunters, y'see,'

growled Butch Mason.

'An' . . . er . . . jest who is it you are huntin'?' asked Hall.

'The Coyotero Kid,' said Payne.

The marshal whistled, while the mayor gasped.

'The Coyotero Kid!' exclaimed Jim Byers.

'Yup.'

'You fellers know what you're takin' on?' enquired Frank Hall.

'Tell us,' said Payne.

'Wa'al,' said the marshal, 'the Kid ain't no ordinary Apache renegade.'

'No?'

'Hell, no! He's been terrorizin' this territory for two years now, an' the joint efforts of the US Army an' the US marshals' department to catch him have failed dismally. Over that period he's murdered 'bout seventy civilians an' twenty or more soldiers. He strikes outa nowhere an' then vanishes into the Chiricahua, or the Dragoon, or the Gila Mountains.'

'Why do folks call him the Coyotero

Kid?' asked Butch Mason curiously.

''Cause nobody knows his real name an' he's a Coyotero Apache who looks to be in his late teens,' said Jim Byers.

'How d'you know he's a Coyotero an' not, say, a Chiricahua or a Mescalero?'

'A coupla survivors of his raids described his war paint. It's Coyotero,' replied Frank Hall.

'They were reliable, these survivors?'

'Yeah. One was an Apache scout an' the other an experienced NCO outa Fort Grant.'

'The Army employs Apache scouts these days?'

'Yup. It has done for some years now,'

'Wa'al, I'll be darned!'

'This Coyotero Kid, he's goddam elusive. If 'n' the Army cain't catch him — '

'Don't worry. Me an' the boys ain't failed yet. Have we, fellers?'

'We sure ain't!' exclaimed Butch Mason

'An', I tell you, we've been after some pretty dangerous felons,' added Norrie James.

'That's right,' affirmed Henry James. 'There was Two-gun Tommy Burns, Crazy Wolf Jenner an' the notorious Bartram brothers.'

'They don't come any more dangerous than them fellers,' stated Payne confidently.

'So, the prospect of huntin' down some seventeen- or eighteen-year-old Injun ain't scarin' us none,' declared Mason.

'You'd be fools to underestimate him jest 'cause he's young,' said Frank Hall.

'The marshal's right. The Coyotero Kid is a natural-born killer an' he knows this territory like the back of his hand,' remarked the mayor. 'You fellers ever tracked down an Injun before?'

'Yeah, there was this Cree renegade up in Wyoming who — '

'The Kid ain't jest any old Injun. He's an Apache,' interjected Hall.

'So?'

'So, you're up against the deadliest foe you're ever likely to meet.'

'But he's a mere youngster!'

'Like I said, don't think he's gonna be easy meat. Youngster or not, he's murdered nigh on a hundred white folks in jest on two years.' Frank Hall smiled grimly. 'The terrain round here is harsh, unforgivin' an' as hot as Hell, yet an Apache can walk or dog-trot some seventy miles in a single day. You boys ain't capable of that or anywheres near that.'

'No, but — '

'A tip. Git rid of them leather coats, else you'll melt out there.'

'Yeah. You're dressed fine for the cool air of Wyomin' or Montana, but certainly not for the bakin' heat of the Arizona desert,' stated Jim Byers.

'OK,' said Jerry Payne. 'We'll take your advice. When we ride out tomorrow, we'll dispense with the leather coats.'

'You ain't aimin' to start lookin' for

the Kid till tomorrow?' said Marshal Frank Hall.

'Nope. We're fixin' to have us a li'l fun tonight, 'fore we git down to the serious business of earnin' the two thousand dollars reward that's on offer,' replied Payne.

'Wa'al, you could do worse than book yourselves into the Desert Fox Hotel. The rooms are clean an' you can have yourselves a bath an' a decent meal. Then, why don't you mosey on back here an' sample what this here saloon's got to offer?' suggested Byers.

'Not much,' commented Butch Mason, glancing round the practically deserted bar-room.

'Not at the moment,' admitted the mayor. 'But this evenin' there'll be poker an' blackjack an' roulette, an', of course, we have some mighty obligin' young gals who — '

'Sportin' women!' roared Mason. 'Now that's more like it!'

The other three bounty hunters grinned. Before setting off on their quest, all of them were eager to sample the delights of good food, good whiskey and wicked women, pretty well in that order. They mayor also grinned. He owned both the saloon *and* the hotel, and he was always pleased to welcome new customers. Avarice had displaced his earlier apprehension.

Frank Hall was less happy. He did not like bounty hunters, men who hunted down anyone with a price on his head. He wished them well, though, in their quest for the Coyotero Kid, yet he doubted if they would succeed where the US Army and the US marshals' department had both failed.

Jerry Payne and his companions took the mayor's advice. Having ridden their horses round to the livery stables, they repaired to the Desert Fox Hotel, where they bathed, changed their shirts and partook of a hearty supper. Then they returned to the Silver Spurs and spent the rest of the evening and part of the night drinking beer and whiskey, and fornicating with the saloon girls. The latter activity took place in the saloon's upstairs rooms and it was not until the early hours of the morning that the bounty hunters eventually retired to their rooms in the Desert Fox hotel.

In consequence, it was noon before the four set out from Sulphur Springs and headed across the desert towards the Chiricahua Mountains. They had strapped their long leather coats to their saddles, but still they sweated copiously as they rode slowly through the scrub and between the various cacti that dotted the desert floor.

Frank Hall watched them go. He turned to find the mayor standing beside him.

'I don't figure those fellers are gonna be claimin' that reward,' opined Jim Byers.

'Me neither,' said the marshal.

As they spoke, the four riders disappeared from view, swallowed up in the desert's shimmering heat haze.

Four hours later, the bounty hunters were deep in the heart of the mountains, bone-weary, sun-baked and drenched in sweat. Their water-bottles were three-quarters empty, yet despite that they were all suffering from parched lips and a raging thirst. Used to northern climes, they had been totally unprepared for Arizona's savage, relentless heat and the sheer desolation of the Chiricahua Mountains. Happening upon a trickling mountain stream, they halted so that their horses might drink. And, at the same time, they dismounted in order to refill their water-bottles. It was then that Butch Mason voiced the thought expressed earlier by both the mayor and the marshal of Sulphur Springs.

'I don't reckon we're gonna git anywheres near this goddam Coyotero Kid,' he growled.

'He was reported as bein' last seen in these mountains,' said Jerry Payne.

'Yeah, but where in tarnation?' rasped Norrie James.

'I thought the plan was to bribe some Apache into guidin' us to his hide-away?' said Henry James.

'It was. It is,' said Payne. He slapped his saddle bags, causing them to emit a loud clinking sound. 'That's why we brought along these bottles of whiskey. It's a well-known fact that an Injun will do anythin' to git his hands on what he likes to call 'fire-water'. It worked when we was after that there renegade Cree.'

'So it did,' muttered Mason. 'But we ain't come across no Apache to bargain with.'

'Not yet.'

'They seem to be kinda thin on the ground, Jerry.'

'All we gotta do is stumble across some Apache village, an' then . . . '

Butch Mason laughed harshly.

'We could be searchin' these mountains for ever,' he remarked.

'Butch's right,' agreed Norrie James.

'So, what *do* we do?' enquired his cousin.

'Wa'al, I gotta confess I figured we'd hit upon a village 'fore now,' admitted Payne. 'Mebbe we oughta git the hell outa these here mountains an' head for either Fort Grant or Fort Bowie.'

'How's that gonna help?' demanded Mason.

'We could recruit one of them Apache scouts the marshal mentioned.'

'Now that *is* a good idea!'

'Glad you think so, Butch.' Payne turned to the others. 'You boys agree?'

The James cousins nodded.

'OK. Then let's git goin'.'

'Which fort are we headed for?' asked Mason.

'I reckon Fort Bowie's nearer. So, we keep bearin' east,' said Payne.

He screwed the stopper on to his water-bottle, attached the bottle to his belt and swung himself back into the saddle. But he didn't quite make it.

The rifle shot echoed through the mountains. The bullet struck Jerry Payne in the chest and sent him crashing to the ground. His companions stood stock-still for a moment or two and then made a grab for their Winchesters. They hastily pulled them out of their saddle boots and scrambled for the nearest cover.

Norrie and Henry James threw themselves behind a barricade of rocks that had tumbled down the mountainside on the far side of the stream. Butch Mason, meanwhile, dropped into a shallow arroyo that meandered through the gulch in which they had stopped for water. As for Jerry Payne, he rolled over on to his belly and attempted to crawl towards the arroyo. He was still several yards short of it when a second rifle shot rang out. This time he was hit in the left leg, the bullet shearing through the bounty hunter's thigh-bone. He screamed with pain and stopped in his tracks.

'Who the hell . . . ?' began Butch Mason.

'It's gotta be the Coyotero Kid,' muttered Norrie James.

'You reckon?' said his cousin.

'Yup. Seems we've found our Injun.'

'Or, to be more accurate, he's found us,' growled Mason.

This exchange had barely registered with Jerry Payne. He was bleeding profusely from both wounds and almost swooning with the pain from his shattered leg. Also, he realized he was a dead man unless he could reach the protection afforded by the arroyo. But, such was his agony, he was quite unable to move.

'You boys gotta help me,' he croaked.

'We make a move towards you an' we'll git ourselves shot for sure,' replied Butch Mason.

'You . . . you jest gonna leave me here to die?' gasped Payne.

'You're darned right we are!' retorted Mason.

'Yeah. Us gittin' killed ain't gonna help you none,' remarked Norrie James.

Payne made no further reply, for he had lapsed into unconsciousness.

An ominous silence followed.

The sun beat down remorselessly and the quiet continued, only occasionally interrupted by the screech of a hawk, several of which could be seen wheeling high in the sky. Did the birds scent, the two cousins mused, that there would be rich pickings later? This thought did nothing to reassure the bounty hunters.

The time ticked slowly by, no further shots breaking the ominous silence. Each of the three chanced a quick peek up at the towering red-stone cliffs in front of them. Nothing moved. Where in tarnation, they asked themselves, was the hidden gunman? Where in that vast open expanse of sun-drenched rock was he concealing himself? The answer was, he wasn't; not any more.

The third shot came from behind them. The Coyotero Kid had plainly succeeded in outflanking his would-be hunters.

Henry James was the next to be hit. The bullet struck him in the middle of the back, shattering his spine. Immediately, Norrie James whirled round, to be hit in the right shoulder. The slug slammed him hard back against the large rock against which he had previously been cowering. Then, as he struggled to stay upright, the Apache's fifth shot demolished his left eye and penetrated his brain, killing him instantly.

Henry James did not long survive his cousin. As he lay slumped against the rock next to the dead man, a sixth bullet struck him in the back of the skull and blew his brains out.

Another period of silence followed.

But this time it did not prevail for long. Butch Mason broke it. Squirming round within the narrow confines of the arroyo, the big man grasped his Winchester tightly and, taking good care to keep his head down beneath the rim, yelled angrily at the unseen assassin.

'Goddammit, come on out an' fight like a man!'

There being no response, he shouted again.

'What in blue blazes have you got against us? We're jest God-to-honest cowpokes on our way through these mountains, bound for — '

'You lie,' a voice from the far end of the gulch interrupted him.

So, Butch Mason concluded, the Coyotero Kid, supposing it was the Coyotero Kid, spoke English.

'Whaddya mean, I lie?' he rasped.

'I have tracked you since you rode into these mountains. You are not cowpokes; you are bounty hunters.'

'Is that a fact? An' jest who are we supposed to be huntin'?'

'Me.'

'An' who . . . ?'

'The white man, he calls me the Coyotero Kid.'

'Never heard of you. I tell you, I ain't — '

This time Butch Mason was interrupted by yet another shot, one which ploughed into the soil inches from his face, sending an explosion of dirt and small stones splattering over him.

'I shall kill you,' stated the Apache.

'No! Look, you're mistaken. Hell, I don't mean you no harm, so why not . . . ?'

Three shots in quick succession sent further showers of dirt and stones raining down upon Butch Mason. He shook his large, shaggy head in an effort to clear his vision. Then, as he looked up, he saw the Apache standing on the edge of the arroyo, gazing down at him.

The Coyotero Kid had been aptly named. A tall, handsome youth, with shoulder-length black hair and haughty, aquiline features marked with black war paint, he looked to be about seventeen or eighteen years old. He wore a faded red shirt, a black leather belt, a white breechcloth and buckskin boots. And he carried a Colt Peacemaker in a holster and a bone-handled knife in a sheath, both attached to the belt at his waist. The Winchester, which he held, was aimed directly at Butch Mason's head.

'Go on, then, damn you! Shoot me!' growled the bounty hunter

The Coyotero Kid did just that, but he did not shoot the bounty hunter in the head. Instead, he shot him first in the right shoulder and second in the left leg. Thereafter, he proceeded to drag Mason out of the arroyo by his right leg. The resultant pain caused Mason, like Jerry Payne before him, to pass out.

When Mason presently recovered consciousness, he found that he and Jerry Payne were stretched out side by side. All their weapons had been taken from them and laid aside. Observing that Payne had also regained his senses, Mason muttered: 'What the hell's goin' on, Jerry? Why didn't the red bastard jest kill us?'

'You'd best ask him,' replied Payne grimly.

'Wa'al . . . ?'

The Coyotero Kid smiled.

'Because I am going to skin you both alive,' he said.

4

US Marshal Pete Bradley and Pinkerton agent Lew Sanders had worked
together before. They had brought to
justice both the infamous bank robber,
Seth Jacques, and the murderous
hold-up specialist, Jake Westwood.
Now, like half of the peace officers and
all of the military in the territory,
they were hunting for just one man,
the mysterious, death-dealing Coyotero
Kid.

Bradley, tall, broad-shouldered and
handsome, and wearing a grey Stetson,
light tan jacket and denim pants, rode a
rangy-looking sorrel, while Sanders,
short, square-built and moon-faced,
and wearing a brown derby hat and
brown city-style suit, rode a lively-
looking grey. Both men were armed to
the teeth. Each carried a pair of Colt
Peacemakers and a Winchester. In

addition, Bradley also carried, in a separate saddle boot, a long-barrelled Sharps rifle, capable of bringing down a quarry at a distance of half a mile or more.

There had been reports of the Apache being sighted in and around the Chiricahua Mountains, the same reports that had brought Jerry Payne and his fellow bounty hunters into the area.

It was late morning when the two men spotted four horses chewing at the sparse grasses that sprouted on the desert floor at the edge of the foothills.

Pete Bradley pulled out a pair of binoculars and brought them to bear on the horses. He whistled softly.

'Wa'al, Lew,' he said, 'they sure as hell ain't Injun hosses.'

'No?' said the Pinkerton man.

'No, siree! They're all carryin' Texas saddles.'

'I don't see nobody nearby.'

'An' there's no sign of any camp-fire. No smoke nor nuthin'.'

66

'You figure we oughta investigate, Pete?'

'I guess so, but let's ride in nice an' easy. An' keep your eyes peeled.'

'Sure thing.'

The two men urged their horses forward, veering off the trail and across the desert towards the mountains. They rode slowly, cautiously, threading between the sprinkling of mesquite and yucca.

As they approached the horses, a small flock of buzzards suddenly flew into the air from behind a hillock close to where the horses were munching. At the same time, a couple of coyotes slunk out and sped across the desert floor, vanishing into a tangle of mesquite.

'What in tarnation?' exclaimed Bradley, reining in the sorrel.

The Pinkerton man pulled up his mount and grabbed the Winchester from his saddleboot.

'I don't like the look of this,' he muttered.

'Neither do I,' rasped Bradley.

'I gotta real bad feelin' 'bout this,' said Lew Sanders.

'Whaddya sayin'?'

'I'm sayin' that mebbe we should jest turn round an' hightail it outa here.'

'Aw, come on, Lew!'

'I mean it.'

Pete Bradley glanced at his companion and was surprised to observe that the Pinkerton man's complexion had changed from a healthy tan to chalkwhite. In all the time he had known him, he had never seen Sanders look so scared. And he had to admit that, when the buzzards had suddenly fluttered up from behind the hillock, he had felt the hairs on the back of his neck begin to rise. But he refused to be spooked by the antics of a bunch of birds.

'No,' he said. 'Let's go see what's attracted them buzzards.'

'But, Pete . . . '

'Let's go.'

The marshal drew one of his two revolvers and slowly rode round the side of the hillock. A patently nervous Lew Sanders followed.

The sight that greeted them was frankly horrific. The bodies of Jerry Payne and his three confederates sat propped up against a large boulder. All four corpses had been skinned and were also partly eaten by the buzzards and the coyotes.

Lew Sanders immediately turned his face away and was violently sick. As he hung out of the saddle spewing and retching, Pete Bradley dismounted.

'We cain't leave 'em here,' he said quietly.

Sanders paused in between retches for long enough to say, 'No?'

'No, Lew, we cain't. Whoever they are, they deserve a decent Christian burial.'

'What's left of 'em.'

'Yeah, wa'al . . . '

'So, whaddya figure on doin'?'

'Tie 'em on to the backs of their hosses an' take 'em to the nearest township.' Bradley thought for a moment, then said, 'Guess that'll be Sulphur Springs.'

'Yeah.'

'OK, gimme a hand.'

'I . . . I dunno if I can,' mumbled the Pinkerton agent, still averting his eyes from the sight of the four corpses.

'I'll do the necessary,' declared Bradley.

'You will?'

'Yup. You jest go git them hosses.'

'OK, Pete. I reckon I can do that.'

Sanders turned the grey's head and headed back towards the spot where the horses remained chomping at the tough tabosa grass growing at the edge of the desert.

Pete Bradley watched him go and then turned to face the corpses. He continued to clutch the Colt Peacemaker as he approached them, for, like Lew Sanders, he felt distinctly uneasy. His instincts told him to run, but he steeled himself to do what he had to do.

Then, just as he stretched out his hand towards the body of the late unlamented Jerry Payne, a shot rang out. He whirled round in time to see Lew Sanders blasted out of the saddle. The Pinkerton man landed flat on his back, while the grey cantered off into the desert, scattering the bounty hunters' horses as he did so.

Bradley ran to the spot where his companion lay. He peered long and hard out into the desert. Apart from the horses, nothing moved. He crouched down beside Sanders and quickly examined him.

Sanders had been shot in the chest. He stared up at the marshal.

'I . . . I told you we oughta hightail it outa here,' he gasped. 'Now it's too darned late!'

'It's OK. Lew. You're gonna be all right. I'll . . . ' Bradley tailed off.

There was no point in his continuing. Lew Sanders' eyes had glazed over and he had lapsed into unconsciousness. Bradley felt his pulse. There was none. The Pinkerton man was dead.

Bradley remained crouching over his

friend's body. Again he peered out across the desert. Sanders had been facing in that direction when he was shot in the chest. Therefore, whoever had shot him had to be out there somewhere. And Bradley was sure it had been a pistol rather than a rifle shot that he had heard. That meant the assassin must have fired it from fairly close range. So, where in tarnation was he?

The area immediately in front of the marshal was devoid of any kind of desert shrubs. The nearest was a yucca some forty or fifty yards away. He rose from his crouch and carefully scanned the barren plain. Nothing.

Pete Bradley, having scanned the area from left to right, now scanned it from right to left. He was half-way through this second search when the Apache suddenly materialized before his startled gaze.

The Indian sat up from the desert floor in one swift, fluid movement and, from a mere twenty feet away, shot the marshal with his Colt Peacemaker. The bullet struck Bradley between the eyes and killed him instantly. Only an Apache or a copperhead could have lain concealed from Bradley's scanning eye on a patch of ground so empty of cover.

The young Apache walked over to where Bradley lay and glanced down at the fallen lawman. He noted the US marshal's badge pinned to Bradley's chest. So, he mused, his latest two victims were peace officers. Were they on his trail, the Coyotero Kid wondered, or were they simply at the wrong place at the wrong time?

Whatever the case, the Kid would not be skinning them. His real hatred was reserved for the bluecoats and for scum like the four bounty hunters, the latter gunslingers who were prepared to hunt down and kill someone purely for a financial reward. Such men he would and did skin, sometimes alive.

However, the young Apache respected the white peace officers, who, although his enemy, put their lives on the line preserving the white man's laws. And since, in common with all his people, he believed wholeheartedly in observing the Apache burial rituals, he felt it incumbent upon him to ensure that the marshal and his companion were buried according to the white man's customs.

It took him some time to capture the grey and calm him down. Then he led the horse back to the desert's edge and draped Lew Sanders' body across the saddle.

This done, he next brought the marshal's sorrel from where it remained on the far side of the hillock and likewise draped Pete Bradley's body across its saddle.

Thereupon, he set off across the desert, leading the two horses and their grisly burdens.

Some time later, he reached the trail a couple of miles short of Sulphur Springs. He found a cottonwood tree beside the trail and tethered the hoses to it. Certain that the bodies would be found by some passing traveller and taken into town for a Christian burial, the young Apache brave then turned and headed back towards the distant Chiricahua Mountains.

Meantime, at the edge of the foothills, the buzzards and coyotes were once again enjoying their dinner.

5

A month after the violent demise of the four bounty hunters and the two lawmen, the Coyotero Kid struck again. This time it was at the homestead of Virgil Parker in the foothills of the Dragoon Mountains. Parker was out front attending to his vegetables and was in the process of watering his pink Mexican beans when the Apache struck.

The frequent raids carried out by the young Apache, their ferocity and their unpredictability, had filled Arizona's civilian population with dread. They lived in a state of perpetual fear. In consequence, the menfolk went nowhere without a weapon to hand.

Virgil Parker was no exception. A short, wiry man in his early forties, he looked every inch a farmer, with his sweat-stained grey Stetson, check shirt, denim pants and well-worn brown leather boots. But, whereas two years earlier he would have carried only the tools of his trade, now he carried a Colt Peacemaker stuck into his belt. Also, he was forever glancing anxiously about him as he watered his plants.

His gun and his vigilance availed him nothing, however. As he paused to wipe his brow, the stillness of that May morning was shattered by a single rifle shot. A gasp escaped Virgil Parker's lips, his eyes widened and he fell backwards on to his rows of beans. He lay there, staring sightlessly up into the azure-blue sky, his heart shattered by that single shot.

The sound of the shot brought forth Parker's family. His wife and daughter came running from the farmhouse, while his two sons erupted from the barn where they had been mending their buckboard's rear axle.

The boys had grabbed their Winchesters and they immediately dropped into a crouch and scanned the scene before them. Their father lay motionless in the bean-patch, the desert, the foothills and the mountains shimmered in the midday heat and the only living thing to be seen was a solitary buzzard wheeling high above the mountain peaks.

Tom, the elder of the two, thought he saw something or somebody stir among the cluster of sagebrush half-way up the nearest of the foothills. He fired: once, twice, thrice. But the reply came from the desert behind him. Another single shot. It hit him in the back of the skull and killed him outright.

Jody, the younger boy, wheeled round, expecting to see the assassin. However, all he could see was the dreary sagebrush desert, miles and miles of it, dotted here and there with cactus, yucca and Joshua trees.

As the boy peered out nervously at the desolate plain, his finger itching to squeeze the trigger of his Winchester, two further shots rang out. His mother and sister had run screaming towards the spot where their fallen husband and father lay. They both now collapsed beside Virgil Parker, their screams suddenly cut short.

Jody swore. The Apache had somehow or other flitted like a ghost from due east to due north. Jody would not have believed it possible, yet it had happened. The boy whirled round and round in circles, desperately trying to pick out where in that harsh, desolate landscape the phantom killer had hidden himself.

Then, all at once, the Indian appeared before him, a few yards away. The sight of the tall, young Apache in his black war paint petrified Jody. He felt unable to move a muscle. To aim and fire the Winchester was quite beyond him. He was completely hypnotized by the Coyotero Kid. The Kid smiled a grim, pitiless smile. He held the rifle by its stock, the muzzle pointed towards the earth. But in his right hand was his Colt Peacemaker. He aimed the revolver at Jody.

He spoke but the one word:

'Revenge.'

'But I . . . I ain't done nuthin' agi'n you!' exclaimed Jody.

'No.'

Despite seemingly agreeing, the Indian squeezed the trigger and blew away half of Jody's face. At the same moment, a bugle sounded. The Kid turned to see a troop of US Cavalry bearing down on him from the foothills to his right. They were no more than half a mile away. Immediately, he set off through the sagebrush, heading for the nearest of the foothills. And, by the time the soldiers galloped on to Virgil Parker's farm, he had vanished.

The troop had, in fact, been scouring the Dragoon Mountains east of Tombstone, several sightings of the Coyotero Kid having been reported from that region. However, after they had spent three fruitless weeks searching for him, their commander, Lieutenant Dan Hudson, had decided they might as well call it a day and return to their post at Fort Bowie. And now ironically, on their return journey, they had stumbled across their quarry. The subaltern brought the troop to a halt while he and his sergeant dismounted and examined the bodies of the farmer and his family.

Lieutenant Dan Hudson was a rosy-cheeked young fellow straight from military college. Sergeant Roy McBride, on the other hand, had almost twenty years' service under his belt. The officer commanding Fort Bowie had deliberately decreed that the veteran should ride with young Hudson on the foray into the Dragoon Mountains, this being Hudson's first independent command. Now, as he gazed white-faced at the corpses, Hudson was glad to have the reassuring presence of the big, tough-looking Sergeant McBride beside him.

'God save us!' he exclaimed. 'Is this the work of just one redskin? Surely he must have had accomplices?'

'You figure it's the Coyotero Kid done this?'

'Who else, Sergeant?'

The sergeant shrugged his brawny shoulders.

'I guess it's gotta be him,' he said.

'And he always works alone?' demanded Hudson.

'Yessir. We've had several sightings over the last coupla years. It's pretty certain there's only this one Coyotero Apache out there doin' all these killin's.'

'And cocking a snook at the US Army!'

'Yessir.'

'How many thousand of us out looking for him?'

'Dunno, sir.'

'He can't be too far way. Hell, we saw him vanish into those hills!'

'Sure did.'

'So, let's get after him. Maybe this time his luck's run out.'

'Mebbe.' McBride indicated the corpses of Virgil Parker and his family with a nod of the head. 'Whaddya propose doin' 'bout them?' he asked.

'What do you mean?'

'We cain't leave 'em out here to be eaten by buzzards an' coyotes.'

'No . . . no, of course not.' Hudson thought for a moment, then said, 'Detail four troopers to take the bodies back to Fort Bowie. We'll take the rest of the troop up into the mountains in pursuit of that murdering redskin.'

'Yessir. Very good, sir.'

The sergeant bellowed out the relevant orders and then he and the subaltern remounted. Moments later, the troop was galloping hell for leather, off into the foothills. Behind them, the four troopers detailed to ride back to the fort with the corpses looked less than pleased. But, then, they did not know what was in store for their comrades.

Having ridden hard and fast into the foothills, the troop suddenly found themselves confronted by no fewer than three separate ravines, all leading up into the mountains. Lieutenant Hudson raised his hand and again brought the troop to a halt.

'Goddammit! Now what?' he muttered.

'The Injun could've taken any one of these ravines,' said McBride.

'Or none of them.'

'Yeah. He could've backtracked. Assumin' he's on foot. If 'n' he was on horseback . . . '

'When we heard the shooting, I think I saw someone run off into these foothills. He was on foot.'

'Me, too. But that don't mean he didn't have a hoss hidden somewheres nearby.'

'No.'

'Anyways, sir, I don't see what else we can do 'cept press on.'

'I agree, Sergeant.' Hudson smiled thinly. 'OK, we split into three columns and each heads up a different ravine. If the Coyotero Kid *is* hidden up one of them, he'll start shooting for sure. Then we'll know in which ravine he's located, and those of us not in that ravine must turn round and make for it with all possible speed.'

'Yessir.'

'I'll lead one column, you the second and Corporal Dingwall the third. See to it, Sergeant.'

'Very good, sir.'

McBride rapped out the orders and within minutes a column of bluecoats was galloping into each of the three ravines.

The shooting began in the ravine into which Corporal Dingwall and his men had ridden. Straightaway, the other two columns turned about and rode to his aid, Lieutenant Hudson's party charging into the ravine just ahead of the sergeant's.

What they found was chaos. Dingwall lay dead on the ravine floor together with no fewer than five of his troopers. The rest were wheeling their horses round and round in circles in a state of sheer panic, firing blindly up at the rim of the ravine. It was evident that none of them had a clue as to where upon the ravine rim their enemy was hiding.

As Dan Hudson scanned the heights for any sight of the Apache, the Coyotero Kid continued to pour down a murderous fire upon the soldiers below. One after another was toppled from his horse and yet, hard as Hudson stared, he caught not so much as a glimpse of the Kid. To the lieutenant's amazement, the shots seemed to emanate from all along the northern ridge. It was as though the Indian was in a dozen places at once. How he contrived to flit from one spot to another at such speed and yet remain quite invisible, Hudson simply could not understand. And now it was the troopers who were the quarry, not the Kid.

'Hell, Sergeant, there's gotta be more than one of them up there!' he cried, as McBride rode up to him.

'No, sir,' replied the sergeant. 'That ain't necessarily so. This Apache's somethin' special. Another Geronimo, 'cept he's a lone wolf rather 'n a war chief.'

'Yes. Well, he's likely to gun down each and every one of us,' gasped Hudson.

'Unless he runs out of bullets,' commented McBride.

'We should never have ridden in here.'

'No, sir.'

'So let's get out. Give the men the . . . aaah!'

The young subaltern hit the ravine floor and lay motionless. In an instant, McBride dismounted and crouched down beside him. Meanwhile, the troopers still fired blindly towards the ravine's rim and the carnage continued.

'I'll git you outa here, sir,' growled McBride.

'No . . . no, Sergeant,' gasped Hudson. 'You get what's left of the troop out of here pronto. Leave me.'

'I cain't, sir.'

'You can and you will. That's an order.'

'But, sir . . .'

'I'm dying. Just leave me. Go!'

The sergeant viewed the officer's wan features, his half-closed eyes and the large bloody stain spreading across his chest. He nodded.

'OK. 'Bye, sir.'

McBride stood up, saluted and remounted his horse. Then, yelling, 'Let's git outa here! Fort Bowie here we come!' he led the charge out of the ravine and back into the foothills.

Eventually, a good mile away from the scene of the massacre, the sergeant brought the fleeing troopers to a halt. He took a quick roll-call. Of the entire troop, only himself and half a dozen troopers had survived.

The ride back to Fort Bowie was a sad, silent affair. They reached it just as dusk was falling and, once he had dismissed the men, Sergeant Roy McBride went to report to the fort's commanding officer.

Colonel Bill Cummings sat behind his desk. Since leaving Fort Bowie as a captain, he had spent several years on the Mexican border, where he had served with some distinction. Consequently, he had gained promotion to colonel and, two years ago, returned to the fort as garrison commander. He looked much as he had when he had previously served at Fort Bowie: tall, slim and dark-haired, though there were now flecks of grey at the temples.

He looked up as the sergeant marched up to the desk and threw a salute. He noted that Lieutenant Dan Hudson was absent.

'Sergeant?' he said quizzically.

'The Coyotero Kid got away, sir.'

'Lieutenant Hudson?'

'Is dead. As are most of Delta Troop. Only me an' six others survived.'

'My God! What in blue blazes happened?'

'The Kid wasn't east of Tombstone like had been reported, but we chanced upon him this side of the Dragoon Mountains. He'd jest massacred a homesteader an' his family.'

'Yes. They were brought in a while

back. So, I take it you set off after their killer?'

'We did, sir. We chased him into the foothill an' up a ravine.'

'You went in after him, Sergeant?'

'Yessir.'

'But he wasn't *in* the ravine. He was up top. Right?'

'You guessed it, sir.'

'Lieutenant Hudson gave the order for you to enter the ravine?'

'Yessir.'

'The entire troop?'

'Yessir.'

'That was not a good idea.'

'No, sir.'

'You should have persuaded him that he — '

'There were three ravines, sir. We didn't know which the Kid'd gone into. We were scared we'd lose him, so we split up an' went into all three.'

Colonel Cummings nodded. He had hoped the experienced McBride would have prevented the greenhorn lieutenant from riding into a trap. But he could appreciate that, given the circumstances, a difficult decision had to be made quickly. Very quickly. Unfortunately, it had been, for Dan Hudson and most of his men, a fatal one.

'Tell me exactly what happened,' said the colonel.

'Yessir.'

Sergeant McBride proceeded to describe in detail the massacre in the ravine. When he had finished, Cummings leant back in his chair and sighed deeply.

'So, Lieutenant Hudson was still alive when you left him?' he remarked.

'Yessir. But he was pretty near gone.'

'Let us pray that he was dead before the Coyotero Kid descended to the ravine floor.' A dark thought crossed Cummings' mind. 'What about the other men you left behind? Were they all dead?' he enquired.

'I dunno for sure, sir. Lieutenant Hudson, he ordered me to git the survivors outa there pronto, an' that's jest what I did. I didn't stop to check up on those who'd been unhorsed.'

Both men reflected for a few moments on what would likely have happened to anyone remaining alive when the Coyotero Kid came down to examine the fallen, as he most surely would have done. The thought of Hudson, or anyone else, being skinned alive was not one that either man bore with equanimity.

'We gonna bring in the bodies, sir?' asked McBride.

'You're darned right we are, Sergeant,' said the colonel. 'We set out at first light.'

'We?'

'You, me an' the whole of C Company. And this time, before we enter that ravine, we send men up top to reconnoitre.'

'Yessir.'

'Not that I expect the Coyotero Kid to be within twenty miles of there. But I'm taking no chances.'

'No, sir.'

'How in tarnation are we ever going

to catch that murdering savage?'

'I dunno, sir.'

'Sixteen, seventeen, or maybe eighteen years old and he has terrified the entire civilian population of the Territory of Arizona, and outmanoeuvred this man's army to boot!'

'Some goddam youngster!'

'You said it, Sergeant.'

'They call him the Coyotero Kid 'cause of how old he is. Me, I'd call him the Coyotero Killer 'cause of *what* he is.'

'You and me both,' agreed Cummings.

6

The hot June sunshine blazed in through the large windows of the conference room in Phoenix's Territorial Capitol building. There were eleven men in all sitting round the table, with the Territorial Governor, Conrad Meyer Zulick, at its head.

Zulick had called an emergency meeting at the behest of Senator Lawrence Simms. He had decided not to call for a special session of the Arizona legislature, but instead to call an executive meeting, together with national representation in the shape of Senator Simms, Arizona's other US senator, Morgan Tomson, and two of Arizona's five congressmen, Paul Jennings and Richard Dalton. The US Army and the law were also represented in the persons of Colonel Bill Cummings and his adjutant,

Captain Leo Vincent, and US Chief Marshal Gus Richards. As for the executive, that consisted of the governor himself, his attorney-general, Leonard Stokes, his treasurer, Floyd Palmerson, and his secretary of state, John Brown.

The last to arrive was the tall, lean figure of US Chief Marshal Gus Richards. When he had sat down and been introduced to everyone, Governor Zulick rose.

'Gentlemen,' he said, 'I have been asked by Senator Simms to call this meeting to discuss the threat posed to this territory by the Coyotero Kid.'

'A reign of terror, I'd call it,' remarked Lawrence Simms.

Zulick glanced at the senator, a small, rotund man with a round, earnest face behind steel-rimmed spectacles. An election was looming in November and Simms was anxious to remain as one of the Territory's two senators. Zulick was equally anxious to remain as Territorial Governor. He was only too well aware that a restless

95

populace was looking for someone to blame for the authorities' failure to capture the young Apache renegade. Therefore, Lawrence Simms' request for an emergency meeting had met with his whole-hearted approval.

'I agree with Lawrence,' he said. 'This unknown Apache, whom we call the Coyotero Kid, must be brought to justice without delay. Barely a week goes by when he doesn't murder someone. And last month he massacred almost an entire troop of US Cavalry. This just cannot be permitted to go on.'

'And how do you propose to stop it, Governor?' enquired Morgan Tomson.

'I confess I do not know. That is why we are meeting together, to discuss the matter and come up with a solution.' said Zulick.

'Wa'al, what has the military got to say?' rasped Simms.

'Yeah, what've you got to say for yourself?' repeated Congressman Paul Jennings.

Colonel Bill Cummings looked

deeply unhappy. Since the massacre in the Dragoon Mountains he had lost all confidence in the Army's ability to track down and capture the Apache. Reluctantly, he rose to his feet.

'What can I say, gentlemen?' he said. 'The Army has sent out many, many patrols, from Fort Grant, Fort Apache, Fort West, Fort McLane, my fort and even Forts Buchanan and Thorn, although they're way out of the Coyotero Kid's range. But all with no success. Searchin' for a lone Apache in this territory is like lookin' for a needle in a haystack. This is his land. He's at home here. We are not.'

'You sound defeatist, Colonel,' commented Congressman Richard Dalton. 'Are the commanders of all those other forts you mentioned equally pessimistic?'

'I can't say, but I imagine so.'

'You are being remarkably frank.'

'Why lie?'

'The colonel ain't no politician, y'see,' grinned Chief Marshal Gus Richards.

'No. Even so, if the military have abandoned all hope of either capturing or killing the Coyotero Kid, where does that leave us?' demanded the governor.

'I didn't say we'd abandoned *all* hope,' replied Cummings. 'We shall continue to investigate every reported sighting, yet our chances of catching him remain slim. Perhaps if we get a really lucky break . . . ?'

'Can't you send some of your Apache scouts into the mountains, to drop into the Coyotero villages and see what they can find out?' said Congressman Dalton.

'Yeah. Mebbe they could persuade their red brothers to betray the Kid?' suggested John Brown, the secretary of state, adding quietly: 'For a price.'

'Or a case of whiskey,' said Gus Richards, repeating the late Jerry Payne's premise, 'An Injun'll do jest 'bout anythin' for a decent supply of 'fire-water'.'

'We tried that,' stated Cummings. 'But there were no takers.'

'That's right,' averred Captain Leo Vincent, in support of his commanding officer.

'Wa'al, even without help, couldn't your Apache scouts track down the Kid?' enquired the treasurer, Floyd Palmerson.

'We tried that, too. We lost five an' the one scout who survived was pretty badly shot up,' said Cummings.

'OK, so the Army has failed so far. What about the various bodies of law enforcement in this territory?' snapped Senator Tomson, glancing sharply at the attorney-general.

'The mountains don't exactly fall within the jurisdiction of any of our county sheriffs,' replied Leonard Stokes.

'When he carries out a raid on some homestead or attacks an unsuspecting traveller, the Coyotero Kid's gotta be within their jurisdiction,' said Tomson.

'Sure he has. But he don't hang about. By the time the sheriff arrives on the scene, he's long gone.'

'So, our sheriffs jest ain't interested?'

'I didn't say that.'

'You might as well have.' Tomson turned to US Chief Marshal Gus Richards. 'What about your people? Don't tell me the mountains are outside your jurisdiction?'

Gus Richards shook his head.

'Nope.'

'So, what steps are you takin' to apprehend the Kid?'

'There are marshals out there.'

'Out there?'

'Ridin' the territory, Senator. Keepin' their eyes peeled. Like Colonel Cummings, I'm hopin' for a lucky break.'

'Gee, this is all deeply depressin',' muttered Morgan Tomson.

'It sure is,' agreed Congressman Jennings.

'Hell, it's more than jest depressin',' growled Senator Simms. 'This murderous young Apache savage has been butcherin' white folks for a period of two whole years now an' nobody's got near catchin' him. 'Deed, the way things are, it don't look likely we'll ever catch him!'

'You sound 'bout as pessimistic as the colonel,' commented his fellow senator.

'I'm not.'

'You're not?'

'No, Morgan.'

'But you jest said . . . '

'I said the way things are.'

'And . . . ?'

'Things'll have to change. We have gotta catch or kill the Coyotero Kid before he murders many more white folks.'

'I agree, Lawrence,' said the governor. 'But how? Have you a suggestion to make?'

'Yes, Conrad, I have.'

'OK, let's hear it.'

'We need someone from the Army's general staff to leave Washington an' come out here to take command of the situation.'

'Have you anyone in particular in mind, Senator?' enquired Cummings curiously.

' 'Deed I have, Colonel,' said Simms.

'And who might that be?' asked Governor Zulick.

'Lieutenant-General Frederick Harriman.'

'Why him?' said Cummings.

' 'Cause he knows the territory. 'Bout ten years back, wasn't he your commandin' officer at Fort Bowie?'

'He was, Senator.'

'Have you any objection to his takin' command?'

Cummings realized that he was in no position to object. Nevertheless, he was not at all happy at Lawrence Simms' choice. He doubted very much that the general was the ideal man for the job.

'No objection' he said. 'But are you sure he'll be willin' to come? I mean, his work at Army headquarters — '

'Oh, don't worry, Colonel,' said Simms airily. 'I have spoken to the general an' he's more than willin' to come to our aid, subject to our invitin' him, of course.'

'Which is the point of calling this

meeting?' said Zulick.

'Exactly.'

'Let us put it to the vote, then,' said the governor. 'All those of us in favour?'

He glanced round the table. All ten present had raised their hands.

'Guess it's unanimous,' said Simms.

'Yes,' said Zulick. 'Can we leave it to you to inform the general?'

'I'll do so immediately I return to Washington.'

'Which means it'll be a little while before General Harriman takes over,' said Cummings.

'A coupla wecks, say. The general will need to clear his desk, but I'm sure he'll git here as soon as he can.'

'I see.'

'He'll wire you, Colonel, so that you can make arrangements to meet him.'

'He'll come by train?'

'I imagine so.'

The colonel nodded.

'I'll wait to hear from him,' he said.

Governor Zulick looked round the table.

'I take it nobody else has any suggestion to make?' he remarked.

The others shook their heads and Senator Morgan Tomson spoke for all of them.

'This was a crisis meeting I had little wish to attend,' he said, 'for I had no idea what we could do to end the Coyotero Kid's reign of terror. Now, however, I feel there is a glimmer of hope. General Harriman will bring a fresh mind to bear on the problem. Also, he's a distinguished and experienced soldier. Just the man to tackle this dreadful situation.'

'Not in my book,' thought Cummings, but he kept his mouth firmly shut.

There being nothing left to discuss, the governor thanked everybody for coming and closed the meeting. Thereafter, they split up; Zulick, his executive members and the other politicians heading for luncheon at the governor's house, while Chief Marshal Gus Richards returned to the US marshals' office and Colonel Bill Cummings and his adjutant adjourned to Brannigan's saloon.

'Boy, do I need a drink!' exclaimed the colonel, as they hurried up the wooden steps on to the stoop and pushed open the batwing doors.

They crossed the sawdusted floor towards the small crowd at the bar. Mike Brannigan, red-faced and genial, greeted them from behind the bar-counter.

'What can I git you gentlemen?' he enquired.

'A coupla beers, please.'

Cummings thirstily downed a great draught of beer and, as he replaced the glass on the counter, chanced to glance along it. At the far end stood a familiar figure: tall, broad-shouldered and wearing a grey Stetson and a knee-length buckskin jacket. The man looked up and Cummings observed the faded blue eyes, the broken nose and the craggy, square-cut features. It was ten years since he had last seen the man. The man's face had aged somewhat and his brown hair was now flecked with grey. But Cummings had no doubt as to his identity.

'Jack!' he cried. 'Jack Stone, as I live an' breathe!'

The big man grinned and sidled along the bar-counter towards the colonel. He stuck out his hand.

'Wa'al, wa'al, if it ain't Cap'n, no dammit, *Colonel* Cummings. How're you doin', Colonel?'

'Pretty well. I'm back at Fort Bowie, Jack, only this time I'm garrison commander. An' this is my adjutant, Captain Vincent.'

'Howdy, Cap'n.'

'Pleased to meet you, Mr Stone.'

Stone smiled at the slim, eager-looking captain.

'Jest call me Jack,' he said.

'So, what are you doin' these days, Jack?' asked Cummings.

'Aw, this an' that. I've jest been celebratin' the end of a cattle drive here in Phoenix. Reckon I'll mosey on up north in a day or two.'

'You been in Phoenix long?'

'A few days.'

'So, you will have heard about the young Injun terrorizin' these parts?'

'The one they call the Coyotero Kid? Sure I have.'

'A bad business.'

'Yeah. You boys don't seem to have gotten anywheres near him.'

'It's not for want of tryin', Jack.'

'I guess not.'

'The Arizona Territory is a harsh, unforgivin' land. He knows it. We don't,' said Vincent.

'I realize that. I was an Army scout at Fort Bowie ten years back. Your colonel was the same rank as you are then.'

'We have Apaches scouting for us now.'

'Is that a fact, Cap'n?'

'It is, Jack,' interjected Cummings.

'That's what your colonel at the time reckoned the Army should recruit. What was the sonofabitch's name?'

'Harriman. Frederick Harriman.'

'That's the feller.'

'He's now Lieutenant General Frederick Harriman.'

'Jeeze!'

'You sound surprised,' commented Vincent.

'Jack didn't rate him too highly. Did you, Jack?' said Cummings.

'Nope.'

'Neither did I. Neither *do* I.' Cummings glanced at the young adjutant.

'This is between you an' me, Leo,' he said. 'I don't want the other officers knowin' what I think of the general. Particularly since he will shortly be based at Fort Bowie.'

'Let me guess.' Stone grinned. 'Harriman's comin' to rid the territory of the Coyotero Kid.'

'You got it, Jack.'

'Whose bright idea was that?'

'Senator Lawrence Simms. Elections are comin' up in November.'

'Ah!'

'Just so.'

'Wa'al. If 'n' the continued presence hereabouts of the Coyotero Kid is liable to cost Simms his seat in the Senate, I figure he's in trouble.'

'You don't reckon General Harriman is the answer to our prayers?'

'I sure don't, Colonel.'

'Nor me.'

'When is Harriman due to arrive?'

'In a week or two, I guess. He hasn't had a formal request yet.'

'So, you don't know what his plans are?'

'No, but I can guess, Jack.'

'Yeah.'

'If only we could catch the Kid before he gits here.'

'That don't give you long.'

'No, it doesn't.'

'Perhaps we should launch one last foray against him, sir?' suggested Vincent. 'It would be nice to present the general with a *fait accompli*.'

'It would indeed.' Cummings turned to the Kentuckian. 'I don't suppose you'd consider actin' as scout on such a foray, Jack?' he said.

'I dunno.'

'There's a bounty of two thousand dollars on the Kid's head,' remarked Vincent.

'I ain't no bounty hunter,' rasped Stone.

'OK. Suppose I reinstate you as an Army scout for this expedition? Pay you the regular rate,' said Cummings.

'I'd need a darned good team.'

'How many?'

'I reckon four at most.'

'Excludin' yourself?'

'Includin' myself. I figure there's any more of us an' the Kid'll spot us comin' for certain.'

'OK.'

'You got three good men, Colonel?'

'I've got a fort full of good men, Jack.'

'I mean real good.'

'I can find you three.'

'Hand-picked, huh?'

'Hand-picked, Jack.'

'OK.'

'You'll do it?'

'Yup, Colonel, I'll do it.'

'Let me git some more beers.'

While they waited for Brannigan to pour them, Stone asked:

'Who have you got in mind? Joe Bailey mebbe?'

The Colonel shook his head.

'No, not the master-sergeant.'

'Is he still there at Fort Bowie?'

'Oh, yes! He retires in December an' I'd rather like him to live that long.'

'You're sayin' this is one helluva dangerous mission?'

'I am, Jack. You wanta change your mind, you'd best say so now.'

Now it was the Kentuckian's turn to shake his head.

'No, Colonel, I said I'd go an' I'll do jest that. This Coyotero Kid's gotta be stopped.'

'Yes. An' preferably before General Harriman arrives here in Arizona.'

'Why is it, sir, that you don't care for the general?' enquired Leo Vincent curiously.

'When I served under him ten years back there was an incident, an incident I've done my best to erase from my memory.'

'It was bad?'

'It was very bad, Cap'n. That's why the colonel don't want Harriman to resume command at Fort Bowie,' said Stone.

'Yes. I'll tell you sometime, Leo, but not now. If the general should take command, it's best you don't know,' added Cummings.

Stone downed his beer. He smiled grimly at the colonel.

'We ain't got no time to lose,' he said. 'Unless you fellers have any reason for stayin', I reckon we should lam outa town jest as soon as you've finished them there beers.'

Cummings nodded.

'You're right, Jack. The sooner we git back to Fort Bowie the better,' he said.

And so it was that, a few minutes later, the three rode out beyond the town limits and on to the vast, sun-baked desert, heading due north.

7

Jack Stone viewed the three men standing before him. It was early morning and he was in Fort Bowie, in the garrison commander's office, with Colonel Bill Cummings sitting behind his desk, his grey eyes serious and his face grave.

'I'm not orderin' you men to take part in this mission,' said the colonel. 'It has to be voluntary.'

'I volunteer, sir,' said Sergeant Roy McBride, his craggy features shaped into a grim smile.

'Me, too,' said Corporal Stacey Grimes.

The corporal looked even smaller than he actually was, standing beside the huge sergeant. Short and wiry, Grimes had fought against Cochise, Geronimo, Victorio and most of the Apache war chiefs. Smart, tough and experienced, Grimes made up for his lack in stature with his proven courage and undoubted competence.

'What about you, Trooper?' enquired Stone. 'Are you volunteerin'?'

'You betcha,' said Trooper Mitch Talbot.

Talbot was several years younger than either the sergeant or the corporal, but, since enlisting five years earlier, had seen active service in both New Mexico and Arizona. He, like Corporal Grimes, was slightly built, yet as tough as old boots.

Jack Stone liked what he saw.

'They're good men, Jack,' said Cummings.

'Yeah.'

'You'll make a good team.'

'We'll need to, for nobody's got near the Kid yet.'

'No.'

'So, when an' where was he last sighted, Colonel?'

'A few days ago, some miles north of Apache Pass. This time his victims were a coupla whiskey salesmen. They were travellin' to Willcox with a wagonload of redeye.'

'If the Kid stole the whiskey, he could be — '

'He didn't, Jack. Not a single bottle. The wagon an' the dead bodies were discovered by a US marshal on his way to Tucson. He contacted the whiskey company, who sent a representative to retrieve the wagon an' its consignment. Much to his amazement, the consignment was completely untouched.'

'Holy cow! That jest ain't natural. It's a well-known fact Injuns cain't resist whiskey.'

'This one did.'

'Yeah. It beats all. Usually, the red man keeps on drinkin' the stuff till he's fallin'-down drunk.'

'Wa'al. It doesn't seem that's gonna happen with the Coyotero Kid.'

'No, Colonel. It sure don't.'

'So, what's your plan?'

'I guess we head for Apache Pass an' then press on, up into the Chiricahua

Mountains. If, instead of ridin' together in a bunch, we spread out an' conduct a series of sweeps through the mountains, mebbe we'll succeed in flushin' him out.'

'At least, it's worth a try, Jack.' Cummings smiled at the four men. 'I wish you success, a speedy success.'

'Thank you, Colonel.'

'You'd best prepare to ride out, then.'

'Yessir.'

The Kentuckian and the three US cavalrymen took little or no time to make their preparations. Just before nine o'clock on that bright June morning they rode out through the gates of Fort Bowie. Colonel Bill Cummings and Master-Sergeant Joe Bailey watched them go. They stood on the stoop in front of the headquarters buildings and the master-sergeant, not usually an imaginative man, experienced a certain sense of *déjà vu*. He recalled the day ten years earlier when Jack Stone had ridden out as scout to the then Colonel Frederick Harriman's expedition against the Apache. That expedition had resulted in the extermination of an entire village of Coyotero Apaches. The revenge exacted had been both bloody and excessive. It had left a nasty taste, and a number of those who had taken part had subsequently terminated their Army careers prematurely. This time there was only the one Coyotero Apache to be exterminated, and both Bailey and his commanding officer prayed fervently that he would be.

The four riders took it easy, for Stone wanted their mounts to be reasonably fresh when eventually they reached the Chiricahua Mountains. If they were to have any hope of catching the Coyotero Kid, they needed their horses to be in good shape. Not that the Kentuckian was particularly optimistic about their chances of success, though he felt they must try. The killings could not be allowed to go on. Someone had to stop the Kid.

It was high noon when they halted

amongst the foothills and, in the shade of some bluffs, partook of a little water and some beef jerky. Then they relaxed for a while, Stone, Grimes and Talbot smoking cheroots while the sergeant puffed away on his pipe. Stone aimed to let the horses rest a short spell before pressing on into the mountains.

'You reckon the Injun's still up there?' enquired Sergeant Roy McBride, peering towards the mountains.

'This is where he was last sighted,' replied Stone.

'He could be long gone.'

'Yup,'

'But you don't think so?'

'No, Sergeant, I don't. I figure he's likely up there somewhere, plannin' his next raid.'

'Wa'al, let's make sure we git to him 'fore he can make it. We don't want no more innocent folks murdered,' growled Corporal Stacey Grimes.

''Deed we don't,' agreed the Kentuckian.

'We gotta take him unawares,'

remarked McBride.

'That ain't gonna be easy, him bein' such a slippery customer,' said Trooper Mitch Talbot.

'It sure ain't,' said McBride. 'If 'n' he sights us comin', he'll high-tail it outa there 'fore we can git anywhere near him.'

Stone smiled grimly. He didn't think the Coyotero Kid would cut and run.

'No, I reckon he'll stay put,' he said. 'His next victim won't be some unsuspectin' homesteader or rancher. He'll be one of us.'

'You figure?'

'Yeah, Sergeant, I figure.'

'Gee!'

'So, we make darned sure he don't spot us 'fore we spot him.'

'An' jest how are we gonna do that?'

'Like I said back at Fort Bowie, we don't ride all together in a bunch.'

'No?'

'Nope. We spread out, half a mile between each of us.'

'He could easily slip between us an'

escape. Half a mile's quite a distance.'

'That's a chance we'll have to take, Sergeant. We must keep our eyes peeled an' if one of us spots the Apache, then he should summon the rest.'

'By hollerin'?'

'Preferably by wavin'. But, yeah, if he's outa sight of the rest of us, by hollerin'.'

'Then we all converge an' — '

'That's right. So, let's git goin'. I'll ride out half a mile to the south, while you remain here, Sergeant. Trooper, you ride out a full mile to the north, an' Corporal, you go with him, but halt at half a mile. Then, when we're all in position, we set forth.'

The four split up accordingly and eventually, when Trooper Mitch Talbot was in position, they proceeded to ride slowly up through the foothills and into the mountains, each of them scanning the rugged terrain for any sign of the Coyotero Kid.

Two hours passed without incident. Out on the northern flank, Mitch

Talbot was wondering what they would do should they not have spotted and captured the Indian by nightfall. The Kentuckian had made no plans to cover that contingency. Talbot determined, therefore, that, as soon as dusk began to fall, he would slant off southwards to join forces with Corporal Grimes and suggest they link up again with the sergeant and the Kentuckian.

However, Talbot had no opportunity to put this plan into action. As he approached a bone-dry arroyo, his horse suddenly neighed and reared up on to its hindlegs. Talbot quickly dropped his gaze, expecting to see a rattlesnake, perhaps. But the cause of the horse's distress was no snake; it was the lance which had been prodded into the beast's chest. And holding the lance was a tall, powerful-looking young Apache clad in red shirt, white breechcloth and buckskin boots, and wearing the black war paint of the Coyotero.

Talbot made a grab for his Army

Colt, but, before he could draw the revolver, the Indian withdrew the lance and thrust it hard into his belly. The trooper gasped and toppled forward out of the saddle. He hit the dirt and, immediately his attacker leapt astride him, pulled back his head by the hair and, drawing a bone-handled knife from its sheath, promptly slit the trooper's throat.

The Apache smiled thinly, carefully cleaned both the lance and the knife on the dead soldier's jacket and replaced the knife in its sheath. Then, he fetched his horse from the midst of a tumble of boulders and returned the lance to its place in the saddle boot next to that holding his Winchester. Thereafter, he set about calming the trooper's horse. And, this done, he draped Talbot's body across the saddle and tied him on, using strips of rawhide.

One down and three to go. The Coyotero Kid, mounted his horse and set off in search of his next victim.

Corporal Stacey Grimes entered the

narrow ravine with some trepidation. He had lost sight of Trooper Talbot half an hour earlier. Now, as he rode into the mouth of the ravine, Sergeant McBride disappeared from view. Grimes hoped he would spy the sergeant once more when presently he emerged from its far end. Cautiously, he urged his horse forward.

The corporal was half-way up the ravine when, without warning, his quarry suddenly leapt from its rim to land on his shoulders and knock him clean out of the saddle. The unexpectedness and the force of this attack combined to render him temporarily defenceless. And, before he could recover, the Apache plunged the razor-sharp blade of his bone-handled knife deep between his ribs. The fierce upward thrust penetrated Grimes' heart and, as he opened his mouth to scream, a fountain of blood gushed forth, choking back his cry. Then, following a second upward thrust, his eyes glazed over, he shuddered convulsively and, finally, he lay quite still.

Two down and two to go. The Coyotero Kid draped the corporal's body across his saddle, tied him on and led the horse up the ravine to where he had left Mitch Talbot's horse hobbled. Thereupon, he mounted his own horse and proceeded to lead both soldiers' horses up a winding mountain path to the plateau which topped the large mesa ahead of him.

It was there that Sergeant Roy McBride found them. He had struggled up another steeply winding mountain path beneath the scorching sun and, with some relief, had ridden out on to the plateau. Mopping his brow, he peered anxiously about him and observed the two horses standing in the shadow of a huge finger of rock which jutted up from the plateau, two hundred yards away to his left. A second, rather more penetrating gaze revealed the two corpses of his erstwhile comrades-in-arms slung across their saddles. McBride swore roundly and cantered across the plateau towards them.

He was not more than twenty yards away when the young Apache brave stepped out from behind the large finger of rock. The Indian held a Winchester in the crook of his arm and the muzzle was pointed directly at the sergeant.

McBride went for his Army Colt, but, before his hand could reach and unbutton the holster, the Apache squeezed the trigger. The bullet entered McBride's forehead plumb in the centre and exited from the back of his skull in a cloud of blood, brains and bone. He was dead before he hit the ground.

Half a mile away to the south, Jack Stone reined in his bay gelding upon hearing the rifle shot. He, too, was on his way up on to the plateau. He listened intently for some moments, then spurred on his horse. As he galloped up on to the floor of the plateau, Stone drew his Frontier Model

Colt. His gaze swept the vast flatness of the hill-top. The plateau was entirely featureless apart from the one finger of rock rising up some thirty or forty feet into the sky.

Stone was quick to observe the three horses, two bearing uniformed corpses. The third stood nearby, the dead sergeant lying at its feet. Of the soldiers' killer there was no sign.

The Kentuckian slowly, cautiously, rode across the plateau in their direction. However, instead of approaching them directly, he chose to circle both them and the finger of rock. Stone half-expected to discover the Coyotero Kid, whom he assumed to be the killer, on the far side of the rock. But he found only the Indian's pony. He glanced at the rock's precipitous sides. Surely no man could possibly scale them?

As he drew close to where McBride lay dead, he was given his answer. A single shot rang out, the bullet digging up the sand only a couple of feet in front of him. Stone looked up and there, on the very summit of the finger of rock, stood the Apache, his Winchester aimed at the Kentuckian.

Stone still clutched his Frontier Model Colt. There was no way, though, that he could raise and aim the revolver before the Indian squeezed the trigger of his rifle. Besides, while he was well within range of the Winchester, his enemy was outside the range of the Colt.

'Drop the gun,' said the Apache.

Stone hesitated.

'Drop it or I will kill you,' added the Apache.

'You're gonna kill me anyway,' growled Stone.

'No.'

Stone gazed in surprise at the young Indian. His mind was in a whirl. The brave had killed three tough, seasoned soldiers and climbed an apparently unclimbable finger of rock, seemingly in full view of, yet unseen by, Stone. Shades of Geronimo in his prime. And now he was saying he did not intend to kill the Kentuckian. Why in hell wouldn't he?

Stone dropped the Colt back into its holster.

'So, you ain't gonna kill me?' he rasped. 'You got some reason to spare me?' he asked curiously.

'I owe you my life.'

'You do what?'

'Ten years ago there was a massacre. The bluecoats came and killed everyone in my village. Everyone except me.'

'Goddammit, you're — '

'Chie, son of Janos.'

'Wa'al, I'll be darned!' exclaimed Stone, adding, 'I didn't introduce myself at the time, but my name's Stone, Jack Stone.'

'It is fortunate, Mr Stone, that I should recognize you before I could squeeze the trigger.'

Stone nodded. He had changed more than a little in those ten years. It was fortunate indeed that Chie had recognized him.

'You speak pretty good English,' he commented.

'Skinya sent me to the mission school at Fort Grant to learn the white man's tongue,' explained Chie.

'You *wanted* to learn the white man's tongue?' exclaimed Stone.

'It is useful to know the language of your enemy.'

'I see.' So this was why Chie, or the Coyotero Kid, as he was known to white folks, had begun slaughtering them, men, women and children. He had reached manhood and straightaway embarked upon a campaign of revenge. 'The folks you've killed didn't have nuthin' to do with that massacre,' remarked Stone.

'My people, too, were innocent.'

'There were some bucks from your village who weren't. They — '

'My father would have handed them over for trial.'

'Mebbe.'

'He was not given the chance, Mr Stone.'

'No.'

'The bluecoats slaughtered not only our braves, but also our women and children.'

'Yeah.'

'Therefore, I do the same.'

'Two wrongs don't make a right, Chie.'

'It is a saying of the white man?'

'Yup.'

'So is: an eye for an eye and a tooth for a tooth. This is from your Holy Bible.'

Stone could not deny it.

'I s'pse,' he said. 'Yet you cain't kill all of us.'

'I can kill many.'

'You ain't plannin' to stop at, say, one hundred or . . . ?'

'No.'

'Jeeze!'

'You and I, Mr Stone, we are even.'

'I guess so.'

'Therefore, you are free to go. And you may take the bodies of your friends with you.'

'Look, Chie, surely — '

'Go.'

'But — '

'Go.'

'OK.'

Stone shrugged his shoulders. He could see that the young Apache was quite implacable.

Under Chie's watchful eye, the Kentuckian dismounted and began to drape McBride across the saddle of his horse. Then, using several lengths of cord, he lashed the sergeant to the saddle and linked up all three horses. This done, he remounted and gazed up at the Apache.

'You go now,' said Chie. 'And do not come back into these mountains. If you come again looking for me, I will kill you.'

Stone tightened his grip on the leading horse's reins.

'So long, Chie.'

'Goodbye, Mr Stone.'

The Kentuckian dug his heels into the gelding's flanks and headed back the way he had come, followed by the three Army horses and their dead riders. He figured that he would be lucky to reach Fort Bowie before nightfall.

8

Colonel Bill Cummings was in his quarters, enjoying supper with his wife and two young daughters when Lieutenant Tom Gibbs, the duty officer, tapped on his door. A voice from within bade the subaltern enter.

Gibbs was twenty years old and new to the post. So far, he had seen no action. White-faced and trembling, he pushed open the door and stepped inside.

He faced the colonel and his wife.

'Sorry to intrude, sir,' he gasped. 'And my apologies to you, ma'am, but the colonel should know that . . . that the detail he sent out this morning into the Chiricahua Mountains has returned.'

'You talkin' about Mr Stone an' the others?' enquired Cummings.

'Yessir.'

'Have they taken the Coyotero Kid?'

'No, sir.'

'Then why in blue blazes have they returned? They've only been gone a few hours.'

'Yessir. You'd best come, I think. Mr Stone will explain.'

'Oh, very well, Lieutenant!' Cummings studied the subaltern's unnaturally pale features and then, all at once, guessed. 'It's not gone well?' he said quietly.

'No, sir.'

'Excuse me, my dears,' said Cummings to his wife and daughters and, quickly rising, he left the table and followed Lieutenant Tom Gibbs out into the night.

'Mr Stone is in your office, sir,' Gibbs informed him.

'And the others?' he asked.

'They . . . they're in the hospital.'

'In the hospital! Are they wounded?'

'No, sir, not exactly.'

'What do you mean, Lieutenant, not exactly?'

'They are all dead, sir.'

'Oh, my God!'

With a heavy heart, Cummings mounted the wooden steps and entered his office. Jack Stone was standing in the centre of the room beneath a kerosene lamp, his face drawn and grim. Cummings turned to the subaltern.

'You may leave us, Lieutenant.'

'Very good, sir.'

Once Gibbs had departed, closing the door behind him, the colonel walked across and embraced the Kentuckian. Then, motioning Stone to take a seat, he went behind his desk and dropped into his usual chair.

'So, tell me what happened, Jack?' he said.

'The Coyotero Kid killed all three of 'em, McBride, Grimes an' Talbot.'

'How?'

'I dunno the details.'

'You weren't together at the time?'

'No,' said Stone, and he went on to explain how they had spread out in their quest for the Apache. Then he described finding the corpses up on the plateau.

'An' the Coyotero Kid? Had he just vanished?' enquired Cummings.

'No, Colonel. He stood atop a rock lookin' down on us, his Winchester aimed directly at me.'

'Yet you're here to tell the tale!'

'Yup.'

'So, how come he didn't kill you, too?'

'He owed me.'

'Owed you?' The colonel's brows contracted in puzzlement. 'I don't understand,' he said.

'The Coyotero Kid is Chie, son of Janos.'

'Janos!'

'You remember the massacre?'

'I am unlikely ever to forget it. That was not soldiers' work. It was cold-blooded murder, in which I was forced to participate, God help me!'

'General Harriman didn't see it that way.'

'No.'

'An entire village wiped out. Or nearly.'

'The whole village *was* wiped out.'

'Apart from Cie.'

'The son of the chief?'

'Yup.'

'I don't recall anyone bein' spared, not even the children. An' I suppose Chie was a child at the time?'

''Bout eight years old, I reckon. He was playin' up above the village. Near where I chose to watch the massacre. I took him to a neighbourin' village to be cared for.'

'I see. An' now he's reached man-hood, he is exactin' revenge for that massacre.'

'That's 'bout it. He's on the ven-geance trail, killin' as many white folks as he can.'

'But he can't hope to kill all of us!'

'He can try.'

'If you hadn't taken him to that village — '

'He might've escaped anyways.'

'I don't think so. Harriman had us scour the area surroundin' Janos's village. We'd have found him for sure.'

'Mebbe.'

'Well, *he* seems to think you saved his life. Otherwise, why would he have spared yours?'

'He wouldn't.'

'You bear a heavy responsibility.'

'I simply saved an eight-year-old boy from bein' butchered. I didn't turn him into some kinda avengin' angel. Harriman did that.'

Cummings sighed.

'Yes; you're right, Jack. It all comes back to the general.'

'When is he due here?'

'One week from today, July the seventh.'

'He's in no tearin' hurry, then.'

'He says he has some administrative matters to attend to first, but I reckon he doesn't want to miss the Independence Day celebrations in Washington. Dinner with the President, that kind of thing.'

'Oh, so he dines at the White House, does he?'

'So rumour has it. He married a Southern senator's daughter who happens to be very friendly with Grover Cleveland's wife.'

'That cain't have done his career any harm.'

'It hasn't.'

'Ironic, ain't it, that the feller whose actions turned Chie into a killer should be the one chosen to hunt him down?'

'Yes. It's also ironic that he has chosen July the seventh to return to Fort Bowie. That is the very day on which the massacre of Chie's people took place.'

'Hell, so it is!' exclaimed Stone. He sighed and then asked: 'D'you know what the general's plans are?'

'I do, Jack.'

'You gonna tell me?'

'I have received orders from the general, outlinin' his plans, but instructin' me to keep them secret.'

'Oh!'

139

'Yes; he wants me to convene a meeting, here at Fort Bowie, of all the garrison commanders in the territory. Then, at that meeting, he proposes to announce his plan of campaign.'

'An' jest when is this meetin' due to take place?'

'July the eighth, the day after his arrival.'

'I s'pose he'll be bringin' several members of his staff with him?'

'No, he's comin' alone.'

'Really? You sure 'bout that?'

'Yes. He is to arrive by train at Bowie Station, at noon on the seventh. He has instructed me to have an escort at the station to meet him an' accompany him to the fort. A first-class horse, preferably a stallion, is to be there in readiness for him to ride. Only the one horse was requested.'

'So, there can be no staff accompanyin' him.'

'Exactly.'

'An' you say his plan of campaign is to be kept secret until the eighth, when he will reveal it to the other garrison commanders?'

'That's right. Jack.'

'But you already know what it is?'

'Yes. The general chose to divulge it to me when he sent me his orders. As Fort Bowie is to be his command centre and is currently under my command, I suppose he felt it only right to let me know what he has in mind.'

'An' jest what has he in mind, Colonel?'

'I told you, it's secret.'

'Aw, come on!'

'I can't, Jack.'

''Course you can. I ain't gonna tell nobody.'

'No; really, I — '

'Then let me guess.'

'OK.'

'As I recall, the sonofabitch is a real evil bastard.'

'Well, I wouldn't go as far as — '

'I would. He had no compunction 'bout murderin' women an' children. So, what's he proposin' to do this time?

Massacre every goddam last Coyotero Apache?'

'Not exactly.'

'No?'

'No.' Cummings groaned. 'OK, Jack,' he said, 'I'll tell you what General Harriman has in mind. But you must promise not to reveal a word of this to a living soul.'

'You have my solemn promise, Colonel.'

'Very well. The plan is this: each garrison is to send a detail into the nearest Apache village, be it Coyotero, Chiricahua, Mescalero, Tonto or whatever. Then they're each to grab a dozen braves an' bring them back to their respective forts. But before they ride out of the village, the leader of each detail is to tell the relevant Apache chief that failure to deliver the Coyotero Kid into US Army custody within ten days will result in the dozen braves bein' hanged by their necks until they are dead.'

'Holy cow!'

'It just might work.'

'Or it might provoke a war with the entire Apache nation.'

'Yes.'

'That's takin' one helluva risk!'

'It is. When Geronimo went on the rampage, we had only the Chiricahua Apaches to contend with, and that was bad enough.'

'Yet I don't see Geronimo gittin' hisself involved in no new Apache war.'

'Me neither, Jack. His fightin' days are over.'

'An' the other war chiefs are dead.'

'But who's to say that one of the current crop won't take on that mantle?'

'Like Cochise, an' Geronimo, an' the others did in their time?'

'Yes.'

'Wa'al, it's possible, Colonel.'

'I simply don't believe the Apaches will acquiesce to General Harriman's demand. Chie is one of their own an' they're a proud people.'

'Yup.'

'They'll find someone to lead them into war, mark my words.'

'Mebbe Chie hisself?'

'No, Jack, I don't think so. He's too young.'

'Yeah, guess so.'

'Anyway, what we need to do is capture him before General Harriman arrives.'

'We've already tried that. With catastrophic results.'

Cummings grimaced.

'I know, Jack, I know. But if we don't try again . . . '

'You askin' me to head another expedition into the Chiricahua Mountains? You wanta lose some more of your men?'

'No, of course not. However, should the general provoke a full-scale Apache war . . . '

'You're gonna lose plenty of your men for sure.'

'Precisely.'

Cummings shook his head, and the two men sat quietly for some minutes, contemplating the dire situation in which they found themselves.

At last the Kentuckian spoke.

'We got one week, you say.'

'Yes. By this time on the seventh, the general will be here at Fort Bowie, all primed up an' ready to issue his orders on the following day.'

'Wa'al, mebbe, jest mebbe I can persuade the Coyotero Kid to stop the killin's.'

'How in blue blazes, do you propose . . . ?'

'Never mind how, Colonel. Let's jest say I got me an idea which might work.'

'But, even if it does, how will you convince General Harriman that the Kid has forsaken the vengeance trail? He will want more than a mere affidavit. Unless you intend bringin' Chie in?'

'Nope. I doubt I could even if I wanted to.'

'So?'

'If I can persuade Chie to stop, I

don't reckon Harriman will pose a problem.'

'Aw, come on, Jack! You said yourself that the general is an evil bastard. He — '

'Won't pose a problem, I promise you.'

'Your plan . . . ?'

'You don't wanta know, Colonel.'

'I don't?'

'No.'

Cummings regarded the Kentuckian with a cool, appraising stare. He noted that Stone's faded blue eyes were ice-cold and his visage grim. He didn't know what Stone intended, but he concluded that it was probably best he didn't know.

'OK, Jack,' he said. 'We'll play it your way. I pray to God your plan works.'

'You do that. I need all the help I can git.' Stone smiled thinly. 'I'm whacked, Colonel,' he said. 'Guess I'll git me somethin' to eat an' then find a billet for the night. I intend settin' out at first light.'

Stone was as good as his word. He left on the following morning, as the sun was just rising above the eastern horizon. Colonel Bill Cummings was there to see him ride out. He admired and trusted the big Kentuckian, yet, on this occasion, he had little confidence that Stone would succeed. Nevertheless, he prayed that he might, for the thought of a full-scale Apache war simply appalled him.

Stone headed southwards once more towards the Chiricahua Mountains. At Apache Pass he turned east and, a few miles into the foothills, found he was being surreptitiously watched from several hilltops. He dismounted and proceeded to make a camp-fire, over which he brewed some coffee. He was on to his second mug when a dozen Apache braves rode up and surrounded him.

Stone's evident lack of concern disconcerted the Apaches, who began muttering amongst themselves. Eventually, their leader, a large, burly brave, rode forward. He shouted something in his native tongue. Stone smiled and shook his head.

' 'Fraid I don't know your dialect. D'you speak English?'

There was a short pause before the Apache replied: 'Yes.'

'Good! An' are you Coyotero or Chiricahua?' enquired Stone.

'Coyotero.'

'Ah! An' who's your chief?'

'Skinya.'

Stone could scarcely believe his luck. It had been his intention to track down Chie's uncle, but he had not expected to do so with such ease. He had headed into the territory where Skinya had lived ten years earlier, hoping that he was still somewhere in the vicinity. His aim had been to attract the curiosity of any Indians in the area and, when they contacted him, as he knew they would, to ask them to point him in the direction of Skinya's village. What he had not expected was that the first Apaches to approach him should be from that very village.

'Will you take me to Skinya?' he asked

Again there was much muttering amongst the Apaches. And again, when they had finished, it was their leader who spoke for them.

'Why do you want to speak with Skinya?' he demanded.

'Skinya is my friend.'

'No. We do not know you. If Skinya was your friend — '

'From long ago.'

'How long ago?'

'Ten years.'

'Hmm.' The big Apache considered Stone's response. Eventually he said: 'We will take you.'

Stone broke camp, remounted the gelding and, escorted by the braves, set forth for the Coyotero village.

The ride through the Chiricahua Mountains was both tough and tortuous. The sun beat down relentlessly and, although it seemed hardly to affect the Indians, it caused the Kentuckian to sweat profusely. At the end of three hours' riding he was almost exhausted and mighty glad indeed to ride into Skinya's village.

He immediately recognized the Coyotero chief, for Skinya had changed little during the ten years since last they had met. He was a mite greyer and his face rather more lined, but that was all.

'You don't remember me, do you,' said Stone.

Skinya stared hard at the Kentuckian, his keen eyes boring into those of his visitor. Then, all at once, he smiled.

'You are the white man who brought Chie, son of Janos, to my village,' he said.

'That's right. I didn't introduce myself at the time, but the name's Stone.'

'You are welcome, Mr Stone. It was a kind act you did that day.'

''Bout ten years ago.'

'Yes.'

'Chie is now a man, a brave.'

'Yes.'

'But he is not here. He has left your village.'

'Yes, he has left.'

'To conduct a one-man war against us white folks.'

'He wants revenge for what happened that day.'

'I can understand that. But he cain't hope to kill all of us.'

'He can try, Mr Stone.'

'I want him to stop, Skinya.'

'Yes.'

'For the sake of both our peoples.'

'For our sake! How?'

'The man who ordered that massacre all those years ago was a certain Colonel Harriman.'

'I know. He commanded Fort Bowie.'

'Yup. Wa'al, he's now a general.'

'What is that to do with us?'

'General Harriman has been given the task of huntin' down the Coyotero Kid, as Chie is known to the white folks of this territory.'

'I see.'

'No, Skinya, you don't see. The

general is, an' always has been, an evil sonofabitch. He will take great delight in killin' as many Apaches as he possibly can. The pursuit of the Coyotero Kid will be an excuse for doin' jest that. An', believe me, he'll kill a darned sight more Injuns than Chie can ever hope to kill white folks.'

Skinya nodded. He closed his eyes and gave the matter some thought.

'This must be prevented,' he said at last.

'Which is why I'm here,' said Stone.

'You want me to deliver Chie into your hands?'

'Nope.'

'No?'

'I don't figure you're gonna turn in one of your own, no ways.'

'You are right, Mr Stone. So, what *do* you want?'

'I wanta speak to Chie.'

'No words of yours will make him relent.'

'Mebbe, mebbe not. At least let me try. You can find him, Skinya?'

'Yes, I can find him.'

'Then either fetch him here to meet me or take me to him.'

Skinya frowned.

'It may take some time to find Chie,' he said.

'Wa'al, General Harriman arrives in this territory on July the seventh. That is six days from now. If my plan is to work, I gotta speak to Chie at least two days 'fore the general is due.'

'I will explain this to my sons.'

'Your sons?'

'They will fetch Chie here to meet you.'

'I could ride with 'em an' — '

'I feel it is best you remain here.'

Stone smiled wryly. Although the Apache chief had not actually forbidden him to ride with his sons in search of Chie, he knew that, should he pursue the matter, Skinya would do just that.

'OK,' he said. 'I'll wait.'

'You shall be my honoured guest,' said Skinya.

And so it was. The Apache may be a

merciless foe. He is also a generous
host.

★　★　★

It was three whole days before Skinya's
sons could track down Chie and bring
him to the village. During that period
Stone was able to indulge in his passion
for hunting. The Apaches were skilled
in the art and took Stone with them on
their daily hunting expeditions. They
were invariably successful and brought
home a variety of game: burro deer,
whitetail deer, bighorn sheep, jack
rabbit and wild turkey. Consequently,
Stone's hours were filled and his
natural impatience to see Chie was, to
some extent, assuaged.

Nevertheless, the Kentuckian was
mighty relieved when Chie eventually
rode into the village in company with
his cousins.

Chie quickly dismounted and embraced
his uncle. Then he turned to face Stone.

'You want to speak to me, Mr

Stone,' said the brave.

'Yup.'

'Yet you did not come looking for me.'

'Nope.' Stone grinned and added: 'You warned me that you'd kill me if I did. So, I figured it best to ask Skinya to do the searchin'.'

'How wise.'

'Yeah.'

'So, Mr Stone, what is it that you wish to say to me?'

The Kentuckian stared Chie straight in the eye.

'I want you to stop killin' white folks,' he replied.

Chie laughed harshly, his black eyes flashing defiantly and his haughty, arrogant features fixed in a look of grim determination.

'Why should I do that?' he rasped.

' 'Cause, if 'n' you do, I'll give you what you want most in all the world. All I need is your word.'

'You would trust me to keep such a promise?'

'I would.'

'Very well. Tell me, Mr Stone, what is it that you believe I want most in all the world?'

Stone told him.

There was a long, a very long, silence before the young Apache brave spoke.

'You deliver and I shall kill no more of your people. You have the solemn word of Chie, son of Janos.'

Stone nodded.

'OK,' he said. 'That's good enough for me.'

'So, when and where will you deliver?'

'Three days from now. As to where . . . ' He shrugged his shoulders. 'You say where. That way, you'll know I ain't tryin' to lead you into a trap.'

'Finger Rock.'

'Finger Rock?'

'Where we last met.'

Stone scowled. He recalled the finger of rock, jutting up from the floor of the plateau, and the young Apache standing on top of it, his Winchester trained on

Stone. Chie's name for it could not have been more apposite, though Stone had no wish to revisit the spot where he had discovered the corpses of his three companions. However, needs must.

'OK,' he said. 'We rendezvous at Finger Rock.'

The Apache and the Kentuckian thereupon shook hands and the bargain was sealed.

9

Corporal Mo Burns was a bear of a man and, like the grizzly, had a fierce, unpredictable temper. Indeed, it was because of his uncertain temper that he had failed to reach the rank of sergeant. He had been promoted and demoted no fewer than four times in the seven years he had so far served, due to his predilection for involving himself in unseemly brawls. A good soldier in battle, he had recently redeemed himself in an action against a band of hostile Mescalero Indians, and, consequently, had once more been elevated to the rank of corporal.

Not one to learn from past mistakes and experiences, Burns was quite as likely to lose his stripes as keep them. He and several of his fellow soldiers had left the fort that evening and ridden into the small desert town of Bowie, intent on having a good time. For most that meant enjoying beer, whiskey and women. For Burns it also meant looking for trouble. In truth, it took only a few beers to turn the corporal into a rampaging bar-room brawler.

Riley's saloon was the establishment which Burns and his comrades invariably chose to patronize, and Brendan Riley, the saloon's proprietor, was praying that Burns would not smash up the furniture as he had done several times in the past. Riley needed the soldiers as customers and so hadn't banned Burns, as he would have liked to do, for fear that Burns' comrades might boycott the saloon in protest. Indeed, he usually detailed a couple of his saloon girls to keep the corporal sweet.

On this particular evening, they sat on either side of Burns at the large table in the centre of the bar-room, where he and half a dozen fellow soldiers were making merry. There were several other bluecoats in the bar-room, but no group was making quite so much noise as the group seated round that centre table.

They sang, they laughed, they joked, they boasted, and they drank. Burns seemed to be in remarkably good humour and Riley was beginning to relax. It was approaching the stage when the corporal could be expected to retire upstairs with the two saloon girls. When that happened, his companions would inevitably start looking for similar entertainment, the party would break up and the danger would be over. Corporal Mo Burns always began a fracas *before* rather than *after* his session upstairs with the saloon's sporting women. Afterwards, he had just time enough for one last quick drink before setting off to ride back to Fort Bowie, which he must reach before reveille. Brendan Riley lit a cigar and smiled contentedly.

But the saloonkeeper's complacency was short-lived for, at that very moment, Buddy Walker pushed his way in through the batwing doors. Dressed in a white linen suit, with a green brocade vest stretched across his considerable paunch, Walker was a big, fat, bald-headed forty-year-old. He was also owner and editor of the *Bowie Enquirer*, a newspaper that had been extremely critical of the US Army's failure to apprehend the Coyotero Kid.

As he ordered a whiskey at the bar, the newspaperman idly cast his eye round the room. Eventually his gaze rested upon those sitting round the centre table.

'Look at 'em,' he said contemptuously to Brendan Riley, who had hurried across the barroom to greet him. 'A bunch of drunken bums!'

'Who . . . who are you referrin' to, Mr Walker?' asked the saloonkeeper nervously.

'Why, them no-good carousers over there who call theirselves soldiers.'

'But . . . but they *are* soldiers! Jest havin' a good time durin' their off-duty hours,' remarked Riley.

'They shouldn't be havin' no off-duty hours. They should be out lookin' for the Coyotero Kid, every last one of 'em,' retorted Walker.

'Aw, be reasonable, Mr Walker! Everyone needs — '

'I am bein' reasonable. All leave should be cancelled till that murderin' savage is caught.'

'Yeah, wa'al, jest keep your voice down. We don't wanta antagonize — '

'You may not. Me, I don't give a damn!'

All those in the vicinity of the bar, soldiers and civilians alike, could not have failed to hear the newspaperman's words. However, Walker's views were well known to the bluecoats and, anyway, they had been warned by their officers not to get into an argument with him or any other of Bowie's citizens. The Army was very keen to promote good relations at all times between its personnel and the local populace, and it was keenly aware that Arizona's civilian population was deeply unhappy regarding the Army's lack of success in hunting down the Coyotero Kid. Quarrels and fist-fights between the two communities would not, it was felt, help matters.

Those soldiers in close proximity to the bar, therefore, chose to ignore Buddy Walker's inflammatory words. Had he remained at the bar, all might have been well. But he decided to step across to the table where Corporal Mo Burns and his friends were drinking, and harangue them. He loomed over them directing his angry gaze straight at the corporal.

'Huh!' he snorted. 'While you lunk-heads swill beer, decent, God-fearin' folks are bein' murdered in their beds. You oughta be ashamed of yourselves!'

'Now, listen here . . . ' began Burns, an angry flush colouring his ugly mug.

'No, you listen here, Corporal.' Walker interrupted him. 'There's hun-dreds, no, thousands of you fellers spread across this territory. An' there's jest this one young Apache, the

Coyotero Kid. But can you catch him? No, sirree!'

'It ain't for want of tryin', Mr Walker.'

'Wa'al, mebbe you should try harder.'

'Whaddya mean?'

'I mean, Corporal, if 'n' you spent more time searchin' for him an' less sittin' drinkin' in saloons, you might succeed in catchin' the sonofabitch!'

'Here, steady on, Mr Walker!' exclaimed Brendan Riley, tugging anxiously at the newspaperman's sleeve.

Buddy Walker shrugged the saloon-keeper off and, leaning across the table so that his face was only inches from the corporal's, snarled, 'Mebbe you'd rather not catch up with him. Scared he might do to you what he's done to — '

'Goddammit! You accusin' me of cowardice?' demanded an enraged Mo Burns.

'If the cap fits, wear it,' retorted Walker truculently.

Incensed beyond endurance, Burns finally lost control and lashed out. His huge fist made contact with the point of the editor's jaw and lifted him clean off his feet, dumping him with a resounding thud on to the bar-room floor. He lay quite still and a sudden silence descended upon the saloon.

It was broken by Sheriff Ike Morgan's voice. At the height of the quarrel, the lawman had strolled in through the batwing doors quite unobserved. And he had reached the centre table just too late to prevent its erupting into violence.

A calm, spare man, soberly dressed all in grey, Morgan belied his quiet looks. He brooked no nonsense from any man.

'OK, Corporal Burns,' he said. 'I've had trouble with you before, an' I'm arrestin' you for a breach of the peace.'

Before Burns could protest, a large hand clamped down on his shoulder and a voice from behind him drawled:

'Ain't that a li'l tough, Sheriff? The corporal here was kinda provoked.'

Sheriff Ike Morgan glanced at the

big, tough-looking stranger, who had risen from a separate table and stepped up behind the corporal. Stone smiled genially.

The Kentuckian had deliberately chosen to enter Riley's saloon rather than Bowie's other saloon, the Ace High, since his plan required that he should remain anonymous. Ten years earlier, when still serving at Fort Bowie, Stone had regularly used the Ace High, in common with most of the NCOs and older troopers. Riley's saloon had always been favoured by the younger element. There was little chance, therefore, of his being recognized from his time then as an Army scout. And there was also little chance of his being recognized from his two recent visits to the fort, for, on each occasion, he had arrived after dark and left at first light.

His plan also required that he should pair up with a uniformed soldier, and he had chosen Corporal Mo Burns. Hence his intervention.

'What's it to you?' snapped the sheriff.

'Nuthin'. I'm jest an interested bystander,' said the Kentuckian.

'Oh, yeah? An' who am I speakin' to?' enquired the sheriff.

'The name's Smith, John Smith,' replied Stone. 'One-time Texas Ranger. So I know how difficult it is to keep the peace. I 'preciate bein' sheriff ain't no sinecure.'

'You do?'

'I sure do, Sheriff,' said Stone. 'An' I certainly don't mean to tell you your business. It's jest that, with General Harriman due here tomorrow, the Army must be plannin' some new initiative aimed at catchin' the Coyotero Kid, an' I figure it'll be needin' experienced soldiers like the corporal.'

'Wa'al . . .'

'Like I said, Sheriff, the corporal was provoked.'

'That's true, I guess. Even so . . .'

'He'll be more use ridin' out in search of that murderin' renegade, rather 'n' occupyin' one of your cells. Couldn't you mebbe let him off with a caution?'

The sheriff scratched his head.

'That's right,' said Riley, relieved that no damage had been done to his property and anxious to appear the soldier's friend. 'Everyone's talkin' 'bout the general's imminent arrival. This could be the beginnin' of the end for the Coyotero Kid, an' I'm sure Corporal Burns is keen to be playin' his part in any new initiative.'

'Yeah, I sure am,' affirmed the corporal.

Sheriff Ike Morgan smiled wryly.

'OK,' he said. 'But you step outa line one more time an' you'll be in jail quicker 'n you can say 'shoot'. Got that?'

'Yessir,' said Mo Burns mildly. Having flattened the newspaperman, his anger had subsided as quickly as it had flared up. Now he was most anxious to avoid arrest.

'Reckon we'd better see to Mr

Walker,' interjected Riley.

'Hell, yes!' agreed Morgan. 'He ain't gonna be none too pleased when he comes to an' finds I ain't jailed his assailant. 'Deed, I can jest see the *Enquirer*'s front page!'

'You're the law around here, not him,' said Stone.

'Yeah, I am. An' I agree with you, he was askin' to be hit. Goddam loud-mouth!' Morgan turned to the saloonkeeper. 'OK, Brendan, let's carry the sonofabitch through to your office. Then we'll bring him round an' I'll explain to him how matters stand. If he don't like it, that's jest too bad.'

'Right, Sheriff.'

Riley had two of his staff carry the still unconscious editor across the bar-room and into his office. He and the sheriff followed and closed the door behind them. And within a few moments things got back to normal: drinks were bought and consumed, the various games of chance were resumed and conversations recommenced.

At the centre table, Mo Burns rose and shook Jack Stone by the hand.

'Thanks, Mr Smith,' he said warmly.

'Don't mention it,' said Stone.

'Wa'al, I guess I owe you a drink.'

'In a few minutes, if that's OK. I ain't finished the beer I'm drinkin'.'

Burns glanced at the two sporting women.

' 'Fore that loudmouth came across, I was jest about to go upstairs,' he said. 'You likely to still be here when I git back down?'

'Depends on how long you're gonna be upstairs.'

'Half an hour at most.'

'I'll be here.'

'I'll buy you that drink then.'

'OK.'

Stone watched the corporal head upstairs arm-in-arm with the saloon girls, one redhead and one blonde. Then he fetched his beer from the table where he had been sitting and joined Burns' comrades at the centre table. They were a friendly bunch and he was warmly welcomed into their conversation.

During the course of this, Stone observed a groggy-looking Buddy Walker being helped out of Brendan Riley's office by the sheriff and the saloonkeeper. Walker glanced across at the centre table and said something to the sheriff. Ike Morgan replied and then proceeded to guide the editor out through the batwing doors into the night. Stone grinned and beckoned to Brendan Riley, who had parted from the others at the door. Riley nodded and came across.

'Did the sheriff inform Mr Walker that he'd let the corporal off with a caution?' enquired the Kentuckian.

Riley smiled and shook his head.

'Nope. He was gonna, but I advised against him doin' so unless he really had to.' Riley went on to explain: 'I knew Burns was aimin' to take them two gals upstairs. So, I figured, if he was missin' from the bar-room when Walker came outa my office, Ike could tell him

171

that Burns was coolin' his heels in a cell back of the law office an' he'd be none the wiser.'

'But if he should find out that the sheriff was lyin' . . . ?'

Riley shrugged his shoulders.

'I reckon it's unlikely. All Ike need say tomorrow is that he felt a night in the cell was punishment enough, an' so he released Burns at first light.'

'Yeah. That oughta do the trick, I guess.'

''Course it should. What Walker don't know won't hurt him. An' it won't hurt Ike neither. With an election comin' up in November, Ike sure don't want the local newspaper campaignin' agin' him.'

'No.'

Stone reflected that the sheriff's decision not to jail Mo Burns had, in the circumstances, been a brave one. And he was grateful to the sheriff, since Burns' incarceration would have well and truly scuppered his plans.

The saloonkeeper moved on, for he

liked to keep an eye on all that was happening in his saloon, whether at the bar, or at the roulette wheel, or at the various games of poker and blackjack. And, as the minutes ticked by, the soldiers at the centre table began drifting off upstairs with one or other of Riley's sporting women.

Therefore, by the time Mo Burns returned to the table, only Stone and one very drunken young trooper remained. As the corporal approached, bearing a couple of glasses of beer, the trooper suddenly slumped forward and passed out. Burns ignored him and handed Stone one of the two beers.

'Here you are,' he said genially. 'Thanks again, Mr Smith, for gittin' me outa that scrape.'

'That's OK, Corporal. An' call me John,' said the Kentuckian.

'An' you call me Mo.'

'Wa'al, good luck to you, Mo. I hope that, with the arrival tomorrow of General Harriman, the Army's finally gonna catch up with the Coyotero Kid.'

'You bet we are, John. The general, he knows how to deal with them stinkin' Apaches. He don't give 'em no quarter.'

'No?'

'You cain't treat 'em like human bein's, John. They're jest goddam savages. In my opinion, the only good Apache is a dead Apache.'

'Wa'al, I cain't argue with that,' said Stone.

'You ever fought agin' 'em, John? Durin' your time as a Texas Ranger?'

'Yup. An' I also came up agin' a few Comanches,' lied Stone, whose colourful career had not, in fact, included a term with the Texas Rangers.

'Red bastards!'

'Yeah.'

'I'm real glad General Harriman's comin'.'

'Yeah?'

'He'll give 'em hell! Did you know that he was garrison commander here at Fort Bowie some years back?'

'No, I didn't. So, he knows the territory?'

'You bet he does. An', believe me, he'll hunt down the Coyotero Kid if it means killin' every goddam Apache 'tween here an' the Salt River.'

'You reckon?'

'I do, John. Ten years back, 'fore my time, there was an incident. One of our officers was murdered by a bunch of thievin' Apaches. Young bucks. Colonel Harriman, as he was then, led an expedition to hunt 'em down.'

'Is that a fact?'

'Yeah. He found the young bucks in some village up in the mountains an' figured he'd teach the Apaches that murderin' one of his officers wasn't smart. Slaughtered every man, woman an' child in the village.'

Somethin' I'll never forgit as long as I live, thought Stone. Aloud, he said: 'That was a li'l harsh, surely?'

'No, John, it wasn't. They killed a white man, an' one who was an officer an' a gentleman.'

'Yeah, wa'al — '

'They're jest vermin, John. You gotta

remember that.'

'I s'pose, Mo.'

'This Coyotero Kid is typical of 'em. How many innocent folks d'you reckon he's slaughtered?'

'I dunno.'

'At least a hundred, mebbe more by now? He's gotta be stopped.'

'I agree with you there, Mo. The killin' must stop.'

'I'm partickerly keen to git the bastard, since a few days back he killed my best pal.'

'Oh, yeah? What happened?' asked Stone, adding silently to himself: As if I didn't know.

'Colonel Cummings recruited some ol' friend of his, an ex-Army scout, to lead a small expedition into the Chiricahua Mountains in search of the sonofabitch.'

'A search which ended in the death of your pal?'

'An' his two comrades. But not the scout. Not surprisingly, he vanished as quickly as he'd come. Scarcely anyone saw him. I wish I had. I'd've given him a piece of my mind, Colonel's friend or not.'

'I'm sure you would, Mo.'

'Wa'al, apart from the fact that Stacey Grimes an' me were good buddies, the regiment lost three of its best men.'

'A bad business.'

'I blame the colonel.'

'You do?'

'Yup. It was crazy sendin' jest four men out into them mountains. Hell, that Coyotero Kid, he must know that there territory like the back of his hand!'

'I guess so.'

'Colonel Cummings should've known better 'n to bring in some old-timer to act as guide. How the old-timer didn't git hisself killed, I dunno. Now, that is a mystery!'

'Which only the scout or the Coyotero Kid could explain.'

'Wa'al, I don't reckon the scout's likely to show his face around here no more.'

'No.'

'An' as for that stinkin' Apache . . . '

'I wish you luck in your efforts to hunt him down.'

'Thanks, John.'

Jack Stone smiled inwardly. He had succeeded in gaining not only Corporal Mo Burns' friendship, but also his trust. That he was going to abuse both cost him no qualms. He had found Burns to be an unconscionable bigot and, besides, he figured that his end justified his means.

'I s'pose your friend has by now had a decent Christian burial?' said Stone.

'He has, an' so have the others.' Burns took a drink of his beer and added dolefully: 'Sergeant McBride left a widow an' two young children.'

'Not a happy thought.'

'Nope.' Burns finished off his beer. 'Let me git you another,' he said to the Kentuckian.

Stone grinned and handed the corporal his empty glass.

'Yeah. Why not?' he said.

While Burns was fetching the beers, the Kentuckian glanced idly round the bar-room. Although there were still some drinkers and gamblers present, the crowd had diminished considerably and most of the soldiers had left. No doubt some bluecoats remained upstairs with Riley's girls, but Stone reckoned that many of the soldiers would be on their way back to Fort Bowie. It was a long ride and not all of them would want to arrive there only minutes before reveille. Quite a number would welcome a few hours' sleep.

Stone grinned. The first part of his plan had been to part Corporal Burns from his fellows. This had proved easier than Stone had anticipated. Only the drunken trooper remained, and he was sound asleep. So, now it was time to carry out the second part of his plan. Stone eagerly awaited the corporal's return.

Mo Burns presently arrived with the

two beers and sat down. He handed one glass to Stone and both men drank deeply.

'Ah, I enjoyed that!' exclaimed Burns, adding with a leer: 'That li'l session upstairs has sure given me a thirst. Tumblin' two women takes it out of a feller.'

'I can imagine.' Stone grinned.

'Usually, once I come down, I have jest the one beer 'fore I head back to the fort. But I figure I'd best make the most of tonight,' said Burns. 'Once General Harriman gits here, all leave an' off-duty hours could be cancelled for quite a while.'

'You reckon?'

'Yeah, John, I do. The general won't rest till he catches the Coyotero Kid an' he won't let us rest neither.'

'No.'

'So, here's to a quick an' successful campaign!'

The two men raised their glasses and Stone repeated, 'To a quick an' successful campaign!'

They drank quickly and soon had almost drained their glasses.

'Ah, that hit the spot!' exclaimed the corporal.

'Wa'al, I reckon it's my turn to buy you a beer,' said the Kentuckian.

'OK, John, I guess I've mebbe got time for jest one more beer 'fore I set out,' said Burns.

'Hang on! I've a better idea.'

'Yeah?'

'Yup. Let's mosey on back to my hotel. I've got a bottle of fine ol' Tennessee whiskey up in my room.'

'A real good whiskey?'

'You're darned tootin' it is. Not like the red-eye they sell here.'

'OK, John, let's do that.'

The corporal licked his lips in anticipation. On his wages, all he could afford to drink was either beer or some cheap rot-gut whiskey. He threw back the remains of his drink in one draught and stood up. Jack Stone grinned and promptly followed suit.

They crossed the bar-room, passing

Brendan Riley on their way out of the saloon.

'G'night,' he cried. 'An' good luck, Corporal. You make sure you catch that there murderin' redskin.'

'With General Harriman here to direct operations, the Coyotero Kid's days are numbered, b'lieve me,' retorted Burns.

'I pray to God you're right,' said Riley, though praying to God was not something the saloon-keeper did much of.

Outside in Main Street it was pretty black. Yellow light spilled out of the door and windows of Riley's saloon and of the Ace High saloon further along the street. Everywhere else lay in total darkness.

'Where's your hoss?' enquired Stone.

'Tied to the rail.'

Stone glanced at the hitching-rail outside the saloon. There were several horses hitched to it.

'OK, untie the hoss an' bring it along. You can hitch it next to mine outside the hotel,' said the Kentuckian.

'Sure thing, John.'

The corporal stepped down off the sidewalk and, bending low over the hitching-rail, began to untie his horse's reins. As he did so, Stone stepped up behind him and swiftly drew his Frontier Model Colt from its holster. He reversed the revolver and, grasping it by the barrel, brought the butt crashing down on the back of Burns' skull.

Stone struck with all the force he could muster and the big corporal slumped to the ground as through pole-axed. Immediately, Stone heaved him up and across the saddle of his horse. It took a mighty effort to do so, for the corporal was no light weight.

This done, the Kentuckian led the horse off down Main Street to where his bay gelding was hitched outside, not the hotel, but B.T. Bradford's General Store, which lay in darkness. He then proceeded to remove the corporal from the saddle and drag his inert body up the alleyway that ran between the store and the neighbouring funeral parlour.

It took Stone several minutes to divest Burns of his uniform, including his cap and boots. Taking care not to drop any of these items, Stone retreated down the alleyway and hastily packed them into his saddlebags. He glanced about him. Apart from the circles of light outside the two saloons, everywhere was dark.

Stone retraced his steps. He checked his victim and concluded that Corporal Burns was unlikely to recover consciousness for some little time. By then Stone would be long gone.

The Kentuckian climbed into the saddle and, leading the corporal's horse by the bridle, cantered off along Main Street, carefully avoiding the patches of light.

He rode across the town limits and on to the trail. Half a mile outside Bowie, he took the fork that would eventually lead him to the town of San Simon.

10

Lieutenant-General Frederick Harriman happily exhaled a cloud of cigar smoke. He sat alone in the carriage reserved for his sole use by the Southern Pacific Railway Company. He was a great deal stouter than he had been ten years earlier when he commanded the garrison at Fort Bowie. Nevertheless, after several years of desk duty in Washington, he was looking forward to some active service.

The general had changed trains at El Paso and was now almost at the end of his long journey from the capital. The train was fast approaching San Simon, the last station before he reached his destination, Bowie. Once there, he expected to be met by Colonel Cummings and escorted to the fort.

He leant back in his seat and smiled to himself. His had been a most successful career. His marriage to Senator Dawson's daughter and his subsequent friendship with Grover Cleveland certainly hadn't done it any harm. But even his wife's influence and that of the President weren't quite enough to gain him the position of supreme commander. For that he needed the approbation of his fellow generals. Well, he thought, perhaps a successful campaign in Arizona would do the trick.

In his time, Geronimo had eluded the thousands of US Army soldiers out searching for him. Now, another Apache, a youngster known only as the Coyotero Kid, was doing the same. Harriman determined that, however many Indians he had to kill to achieve his aim, he would bring the Kid to book. And he would take great pleasure in watching the miscreant hang by his neck until he was dead.

While General Harriman was approaching San Simon by train, Jack Stone was riding through the town towards the rail station. He was dressed in Mo Burns' uniform and trailing the corporal's horse. The uniform fitted him pretty well. He had picked on the big corporal because the two of them were much of a size. The cap might have posed a problem, but Stone had been lucky. It fitted him exactly. The first part of his plan had gone without a hitch.

The second part might fail, however, should the general recognize him. Yet it was ten years since they had last met, on that memorable afternoon when Stone had resigned as an Army scout. He had aged somewhat since then and, besides, he was dressed in the uniform of a US Army corporal. Even if Harriman did find his face familiar, surely the general would simply assume he had been a soldier serving at Fort Bowie at that time.

Upon reaching the station, the Kentuckian hitched the two horses to the rail outside and walked through on to the platform. There were a few people awaiting the train from El Paso.

Among them was a railway porter.

Stone approached him.

'Is the train from El Paso on time?' he enquired.

'Yessir,' said the porter. He glanced at his watch. 'It's due any minute an', look, here it is now.'

Stone glanced along the track, to see the train come slowly into view.

'Thanks,' he said.

When the train halted at the platform and a guard appeared, whistle in hand, in one of its doorways, Stone strode across and hailed him.

'Excuse me,' he said, 'but I b'lieve you have General Harriman aboard?'

'We do, Corporal,' replied the guard. 'He has his own private carriage.'

'Could you take me to it?'

'I'm not sure the general will wanta be disturbed.'

'It's kinda urgent. There has been a change of plan. The general was due to disembark at Bowie, right?'

'Yes, indeed.'

'Wa'al, that's all changed. He's to git

off here. So, if 'n' you could take me to him an' then hold the train till we've disembarked . . . ?'

'This train has a schedule to keep.'

'Don't worry, I'll have the general off the train in next to no time.'

'OK,' said the guard. 'Come with me.'

The Kentuckian clambered aboard and followed the guard along the corridor until they reached the general's carriage. Then, muttering, 'Be as quick as you can,' the guard left him.

Stone entered and, standing stiffly to attention, threw the general a salute. Harriman gazed up at his visitor, removed the cigar from his mouth and enquired curiously:

'You got business with me, Corporal?'

'Yessir,' said Stone.

'Couldn't it have waited till we got to Bowie?'

'No, sir.'

'Go on then, spit it out.'

'Colonel Cummings sends his compliments an' wishes to inform you there's been a change of plan. You're to disembark here at San Simon, sir, instead of travellin' on to Bowie.'

'But why, dammit? Bowie's a darned sight nearer the fort.'

'Yessir. Only Colonel Cummings ain't at Fort Bowie.'

'Then, where the hell is he?'

'In the foothills of the Chiricahua Mountains, sir.'

'Indeed?'

'Yessir. He said to tell you he reckons he's tracked down the Coyotero Kid at last. He's hopin' to capture the Injun within the next coupla hours or so.'

Harriman frowned. This would render his journey quite unnecessary and, into the bargain, Cummings would grab all the glory. Or would he? The frown slowly receded, to be replaced by a sly smile.

'Is it the colonel's intention that I rendezvous with him in those foothills?'

'That's right, sir.'

'He wants me to be present when he captures the Coyotero Kid?'

'Yessir.'

The smile broadened. The US Army had been hunting for the Apache for over two years without success. Now it seemed they had located him at last and were about to take him. And he, Frederick Harriman, was to be there to witness his capture. So, who would submit the relevant report to Washington? Not Colonel Cummings. No; he, as the senior officer, would submit it. And he would make very sure that he claimed the major share of the credit.

'Very well,' he said, 'let us proceed.' Then he glanced at the large portmanteau he had brought with him. 'What in blue blazes am I gonna do with that?' he exclaimed.

'Why don't you leave it on the train, sir? There's always a military presence at Bowie station. You can instruct the guard to deliver it into their hands for transportation to Fort Bowie.'

Harriman smiled benignly at the Kentuckian.

'Good idea, Corporal. I'll do just

that,' he averred.

'Then shall we be goin', sir?'

'Yes, indeed.'

Stone saluted a second time and stepped aside to let the general pass. Then he followed him off the train.

'Ah, there you are, General!' said the relieved guard, anxious to get the train under way again.

'Yes, guard, here I am,' said Harriman. 'But, before you blow that whistle and depart, I have some instructions for you.'

'Yessir?'

'My portmanteau. I have left it aboard. You will be responsible for it until you hand it over to the military at Bowie station. Is that understood?'

'It is, sir.'

'What is your name, guard?'

'Stanley Long, General.'

'Well, Stanley Long, be sure you hand that portmanteau to someone in authority, and not just to a common trooper. A sergeant would be preferable, but whoever you hand it to must have, at the very least, two stripes.'

'Very good, General. You may rely on me.'

'I do hope so, guard,' said Harriman, adding pointedly, 'for *your* sake.'

Thereupon, he turned on his heel and made for the station exit. Stone grinned and followed.

The general eyed the two horses hitched to the rail outside the station. He looked less than pleased when Stone began to mount the bay gelding. He stared hard at Corporal Mo Burns' horse.

'That my horse?' he snapped.

'Yessir,' said Stone.

'I asked for a stallion. That horse is a gelding, like yours, only not so rangy-lookin'.'

'Colonel Cummings, he picked this one out special.'

'He did?'

'Yessir. That hoss is real tough an' durable, ideal for this territory.'

'You think so?'

'I do, sir.'

'Hmm.'

Harriman did not look entirely convinced, but he mounted the gelding none the less.

'Ready to ride, sir?' asked Stone.

'I am. Lead on, Corporal,' said the general.

The ride through town took a little while, for news of the general's coming to Arizona had spread from fort to township throughout the region. The citizens of San Simon had not expected him to arrive in their town, but, once he had been recognized, they gathered on the sidewalks to cheer him on his way. The fear generated by the ferocity and frequency of the Coyotero Kid's random killings had gripped entire communities and the good people of San Simon were no exception. News of the general's coming had given them hope and, consequently, they were keen to applaud their potential saviour. Harriman, for his part, revelled in the adulation accorded him and proceeded along Main Street at a stately canter.

Once beyond the town limits, however, both he and Stone urged their horses into a gallop as they headed towards the distant mountains.

The ride was an arduous one, for the sun beat down relentlessly as they sped across the harsh, desolate desert. By the time they reached the foothills a good two hours later, Harriman was sweating like a bull and feeling pretty saddle-sore. He was badly out of condition, the occasional gentle trot around Washington's parks having done little to preserve his fighting fitness. Breathing heavily, he reined in the gelding.

'We got much further to ride?' he gasped.

'No, sir.' Stone pointed to the large mesa directly ahead of them. 'Up there on that plateau. That's journey's end.'

'That's a strange place to find an Apache village.'

'Aw, the Coyotero Kid ain't in no village.'

'No?'

'No. He's a real lone wolf.'

'An' you say Colonel Cummings has tracked this lone wolf to his lair?'

'Yessir.'

'The colonel's sure he's there?'

'He is, sir. The colonel's got the Kid surrounded, but, since you was comin' all this way from Washington, he figured he'd delay movin' in on the Kid till you got here.'

'That's mighty civil of him.' Harriman had always regarded Cummings as a touch naïve. Had their roles been reversed, Harriman would never have waited for the general. 'OK, let's get on up there,' he said.

They rode on for another half mile and then began to ascend the precipitous mountain path that led to the summit of the mesa. It was a tortuous, twisting trail at no point wider than four feet. Good horsemanship, combined with a surefooted mount, was necessary to accomplish this hazardous ascent. Consequently, Harriman was sweating from more than just the heat by the time they reached the plateau.

He peered across its vast, open expanse broken only by the perpendicular column of rock which the Apaches had named Finger Rock. He turned to face the Kentuckian.

'There ain't nobody here!' he exclaimed. 'Where in blue blazes are Colonel Cummings an' his men?'

'Probably at Fort Bowie.'

'At Fort Bowie! But you said . . . ' Harriman stopped as the Kentuckian whipped out his revolver and pointed it straight at his heart. 'What the hell? You . . . you ain't no soldier!'

'That's right, General,' acknowledged Stone. 'I ain't.'

The general stared long and hard at Stone.

'You ain't no soldier, yet I know you, don't I?' he rasped. 'I recognized your face when you confronted me in my railway carriage. I couldn't put a name to it, but simply assumed you'd been servin' at Fort Bowie when I was in command there.'

'I was there then, certainly.'

'When exactly?'

'Ten years back. I resigned straight-away after you massacred every man, woman an' child in that Coyotero village up beyond Apache Pass.'

'Goddammit, now I know who you are! You're that Injun-lovin' scout who led us to the village!'

'Actually, I ain't partickerly fond of Injuns. I jest don't approve of the senseless killin' of women an' children.'

'Nonsense! Those goddam Coyotero Apaches are nuthin' but savages, every last one of 'em.'

'Oh, yeah?'

'Yes. They ain't hardly human. They are vermin, that's what they are.'

Stone smiled wryly. The man whose uniform he had taken, Corporal Mo Burns, had made almost precisely the same comments back at Riley's saloon.

'Wa'al, what you did then is the reason for the Coyotero Kid's current spate of killin's. He's ridin' the vengeance trail,' said Stone.

'Poppycock!' snorted Harriman. 'There

was nobody left to ride the vengeance trail. You said yourself that we killed every man, woman an' child in the village.'

'So I did, but, y'see, there was one eight-year-old boy jest outside the village when you attacked.'

'If there had been, we'd have found him. I ordered a thorough search of the surroundin' area.'

'He was gone by then.'

'Gone! How . . . how do you know?'

''Cause I took him with me an' left him at his uncle's village.'

'Good God! An' . . . an' this eight-year-old has now grown into manhood an' . . . ' Harriman paused while this sank in. Then he cried, 'Are you tellin' me *he* is the Coyotero Kid?'

'Yup.'

'Then, you're responsible! If you hadn't — '

'Shuddup.'

'How . . . how dare you!'

'Shuddup. Someone else said that to

me. But I didn't massacre his people. You did.'

Harriman carefully eyed the gun in Stone's hand. There was no way he could draw his Army Model Colt from its holster before the other shot him. A note of panic crept into his voice.

'What are you aimin' to do with me?'

'Hand you over to Chie.'

'Chie?'

'Chie, son of Janos. You remember Janos, don't you? You oughta, 'cause you shot him.'

'But why are you doin' this?'

'I figured that Chie would wanta git his hands on you, that he'd want that more 'n anythin' else in the world. So, I made a deal with him. I hand you over an' he calls a halt to the killin'.'

'He agreed to this . . . this deal?'

'Yup.'

'An' you believe he'll keep his word?'

'I do.'

'You'll never get away with this. The Army'll hunt you down an' — '

'I don't reckon so. Hell, they don't

even know who I am! The feller I took this uniform off knows me only as John Smith, which, as you know, ain't my real name. Oh, sure, he'd recognize me if he saw me, but, then, I don't aim to stay in these parts. By first light tomorrow, I'll be in Phoenix.'

The Kentuckian smiled. Colonel Cummings might well figure out what had happened, but he had no actual proof and, in any event, was unlikely to say anything.

'Stone!' yelled the general, suddenly dredging up the Kentuckian's name from the recesses of his mind.

'That's right,' said Stone. 'But you won't be tellin' nobody, 'cause you'll be dead. Now move.'

He gestured with his revolver.

'An' if I don't?' said Harriman,

'Then I'll shoot you. But not to kill, jest to disable you. Chie wants the pleasure of killin' you hisself.'

Harriman shuddered, but, menaced by Stone's gun, he had no alternative other than to obey. He set off at a very slow trot towards Finger Rock. Stone kept pace with him.

As they neared the rock the tall, black-haired young Apache stepped out from behind it. His hawklike visage was streaked with black war paint and he held a Winchester, its muzzle aimed exactly half-way between the two approaching riders.

'That is close enough, Mr Stone,' he said.

Stone smiled wryly. The Indian was just out of range of his revolver. Chie was evidently taking no chances.

Both the general and the Kentuckian reined in their horses.

'This is General Frederick Harriman, who shot your father an' ordered the massacre of your people,' said Stone.

'Yes.'

'He's all yours.'

'Thank you.'

'You'll keep your part of our bargain?'

'You have my word, Mr Stone.'

'Good!'

Stone turned and trotted back the way he had come. He was half-way across the plateau when the first shot rang out. It was quickly followed by a second. Stone glanced over his shoulder. The general lay flat on his back on the ground, with the Apache standing over him.

Chie waited patiently until Stone had left the plateau and disappeared down the mountain path. Then, he glared down at his victim.

'Now you shall die,' he said quietly. 'But slowly. I shall take great pleasure in skinning you alive.'

He had shot Harriman in the shoulder and in the thigh, thus rendering him quite helpless. Smiling grimly, he pulled the bone-handled knife from its sheath and commenced his gory task.

The air resounded with Harriman's cries as Chie, having ripped away the general's shirt and jacket, began skilfully removing layers of skin with his razor-sharp blade. Indeed, so engrossed was he in what he was doing and so loud were the general's screams that even Chie's highly tuned instincts were not sufficient to save him. He sensed danger at the very last moment and turned to find himself staring into the muzzle of Stone's revolver. Then Stone shot the Apache dead.

Waiting until Chie was totally absorbed in his act of revenge, Stone had removed his boots and then, using the skills he had learned during his years as an Army scout, had silently retraced his steps up the path and across the plateau. Barefoot, he had moved with the speed and grace of a mountain lion, to catch the Indian unawares.

He was leading Corporal Burns' horse away when the general called out to him.

'You've got to get me outa here, Stone,' gasped Harriman. 'There's a two-thousand-dollar reward for the Coyotero Kid's capture dead or alive. Well, I'll double it.'

'Forgit it,' said Stone. 'I ain't claimin' no bounty an' I ain't takin' you no place, you sonofabitch. You're gonna stay here an' provide meat for the buzzards.'

'You can't do this! You can't leave me, Stone! For pity's sake . . . '

The general's cries followed the Kentuckian as he crossed the plateau and headed down the mountain path. Ignoring them, he pulled his boots back on, mounted the bay gelding and, leading the other horse, carried on down the mountainside.

He had killed Chie, but not because he hadn't trusted the Apache to keep his promise. It was simply that, in Stone's book, two wrongs never did make a right.

WEST OF EDEN

Mike Stall

Marshal Jack Adams was tired of people shooting at him. So when the kid came into town sporting a two-gun rig and out to make his reputation — at Adams' expense — it was time to turn in his star and buy that horse ranch he'd dreamed about in the Eden Valley. It looked peaceful, but the valley was on the verge of a range-war and there was only one man to stop it. So Adams pinned on a star again and started shooting back — with a vengeance!

BAR 10 GUNSMOKE

Boyd Cassidy

As always, Bar 10 rancher Gene Adams responded to a plea for help, taking Johnny Puma and Tomahawk. They headed into Mexico to help their friend Don Miguel Garcia. But they were walking into a trap laid by the outlaw known as Lucifer. When the Bar 10 riders arrived at Garcia's ranch, Johnny was cut down in a hail of bullets. Adams and Tomahawk thunder into action to take on Lucifer and his gang. But will they survive the outlaws' hot lead?

THE FRONTIERSMEN

Elliot Conway

Major Philip Gaunt and his former batman, Naik Alif Khan, veterans of dozens of skirmishes on British India's north-west frontier, are fighting the wild and dangerous land of northern Mexico. Aided by 'Buckskin' Carlson, a newly reformed drunk, they are hunting down Mexican bandidos who murdered the major's sister. But it proves to be a dangerous trail. Death by knife and gun is never far away. Will they finally deliver cold justice to the bandidos?

A BULLET FOR MISS ROSE

Scott Dingley

In the aftermath of a bank robbery in Terlingua, Rose Morrison lies dead. Assigned to pursue her killer, Ranger Parker Burden learns that the chief suspect is the son of his friend, Don Vicente Hernandez. Teamed with a Pinkerton detective, Parker pursues Angel Hernandez to Mexico, shadowed by bounty hunters. They become mixed up with the tyrannical General Ortega and uncover a sinister conspiracy. There is a bloody showdown, but has Parker found the one who fired the fatal bullet at Miss Rose?